Secrets...
& Rivals

D1374463

...*Plus!*

DO YOU BELIEVE EVERYTHING
YOU HEAR?
TRY OUR FAB QUIZ AT THE
BACK OF THE BOOK

SOME SECRETS ARE JUST TOO GOOD TO KEEP TO YOURSELF!

Sugar
SECRETS...

...& Rivals

Mel Sparke

Collins
An Imprint of HarperCollinsPublishers

Published in Great Britain by Collins in 1999
Collins is an imprint of HarperCollinsPublishersLtd
77–85 Fulham Palace Road, Hammersmith, London W6 8JB

The HarperCollins website address is
www.fireandwater.com

9 8 7 6 5 4

ISBN 0 00 675440 6

Printed and bound in Great Britain by
Caledonian International Book Manufacturing Ltd, Glasgow

With thanks to Sue Dando

CHAPTER 1

●●●●●●●●●●●●●●●●●●●●●●●●●●●●

IT'S ONLY A GAME

"Ooh, you're such a good snogger!"

"I know..."

"I've been dying for this to happen for ages."

"Me too..."

"You've got lovely soft lips."

"Mmmm."

"And such a tasty bod."

"Uh huh..."

"And you smell fab!"

"Sonja?"

"Yeah?"

"D'you think you could shut up a minute while I stick my tongue down your throat?"

"OK. Sorry, Ol!"

To loud cheers and wolf whistles from the rest of the gang, Ollie Stanton and Sonja Harvey wrestled each other to the ground and began rolling around on the grass in mock passion. They hadn't had this much fun playing spin the bottle in ages.

It was a balmy Saturday and everyone had gathered at Matt Ryan's huge house in the posh part of town.

As the afternoon turned into evening, Matt had lit the barbie, raided the larder and his dad's drinks store and rigged up his sound system so that it could blare music out into the vast, secluded garden.

Someone had suggested they play silly games and, after a couple of rounds of tag and blind man's buff, they had now settled into the ultimate party game.

When Catrina Osgood had dared Ollie to snog the most fanciable female there, she had really expected him to choose her and was a bit miffed when he didn't.

In fact, fuelled by a couple of glasses of punch, Ollie had grabbed her cousin, Sonja, not because he fancied her – he didn't – but because he knew she'd take it all in good part.

"Eurroouf!" gasped Ollie suddenly. "Son, your elbow's digging into my stomach!"

"Oh, sorry! I can't move though 'cause you're lying on my hair..."

"Oh, right. Hang on... better? Now, where was I?"

"You were about to give her a love bite, mate!" called Matt.

"Don't you dare!" hissed Sonja.

"No way!" Ollie laughed. "She'd knee me where it hurts."

"Too right I would!" yelled Sonja.

"If only Elaine could see you now, Ol," chortled Cat. "She'd dump you like a shot!"

Ollie had a long-distance relationship with Elaine, who lived quite a distance from Winstead, and only saw her occasionally. He refused to call her his 'girlfriend', insisting that it was more casual than that. But even so, Cat had a point. Surely Elaine would be pretty annoyed by the convincing display that Ollie was putting on, no matter how innocent.

And while Ollie hadn't expected Sonja to join in with such enthusiasm, he was pretty chuffed that someone so drop-dead gorgeous appeared to be quite keen on snogging him.

Only Kerry failed to join in the heckling. The sight of her two best friends thrashing about on the lawn was giving her a strange sense of unease, though she couldn't work out why.

"This is looking good!" Matt continued. "Swap places for a fiver, Ol?"

"I'll pay a tenner to see Ollie and Matt snog," Catrina quipped. "That'd be much more interesting."

"In your dreams, Cat," laughed Ollie.

"More like a nightmare," Sonja added. "Now, have you lot had enough ogling? I can feel ants crawling up my leg..."

"Are you sure it's not Ollie?" joked Matt. "OK, the show's over. Well done you two, although I would have liked to see more exchange of saliva. Now it's my turn to ask the questions."

When Sonja and Ollie rejoined the circle, Matt gave the bottle a flick with his fingers. As it spun round once more, Sonja, Matt, Catrina and Ollie shouted excitedly, while Kerry, Joe and Maya watched in silence.

Gradually, the bottle slowed and the neck came to rest, pointing accusingly at... Kerry.

She groaned inwardly. Kerry hated this game and dreaded it whenever one of the others – usually someone loud like Matt or Sonja – suggested they play it. She wasn't the most outgoing person in the world and hated the idea of being asked to spill her guts or undertake some ridiculous dare in front of everyone.

"So, Kerry!" Matt announced dramatically. "What do you want... truth or dare?"

Kerry shifted uneasily in her seat. She knew

that with Matt in charge of proceedings, his demands would be deeply humiliating or really rude.

Or both.

Kerry made a snap decision.

"Truth, please," she announced, as lightly as possible.

"Hmmmm..." Matt continued with an air of drama. "I wonder... what do we want to know about you, Kerry?"

He put his index finger to his mouth, furrowed his brow and looked thoughtfully skywards.

"I know! Is it true that you're considering cosmetic surgery to have your breasts enlarged?"

His question had the desired effect. Sonja and Maya gasped out loud, the boys looked down at the grass, embarrassed, and Kerry blushed furiously.

Sometimes she hated Matt. He knew exactly which buttons to push to cause her the utmost humiliation. Although she'd never spoken to him about it (like, *as if*), somehow he obviously knew she had a thing about the size of her boobs (or rather, lack of them).

Her 34-inch chest with its A-cup bra had been the bane of Kerry's life in recent years. And at sixteen, she had practically given up on the notion that she might ever sprout proper boobs, believing deep down that if it was going to happen it would have done so by now.

Sure, she had a hang-up about them, but it wasn't something she harped on about or even admitted to in public. The fact that Matt had taken this moment to point out her childlike chest to the entire world caused Kerry considerable embarrassment.

She had three options. Refuse to answer and therefore be expected to carry out some equally cringe-making forfeit, answer truthfully... or lie.

Kerry chose the final option. There was no way she was going to give Matt the satisfaction of causing her any more embarrassment.

"I'm p-perfectly happy with my chest, thank you very much," she stammered, thinking *I mustn't let him get to me*. "So the answer is a most definite no."

"Anyway," Ollie chipped in, winking at Kerry, "more than a handful is a waste, that's what I say."

Everyone laughed and Kerry smiled, grateful to Ollie for taking the pressure off her.

"Right, my turn to do the spinning," Sonja called, grabbing the bottle and flicking it with her fingers so that it whizzed across the grass at great speed and landed right in front of Matt.

"Ooh, I think that must mean it's your turn Matt," Sonja grinned wickedly.

She and Matt were good mates and knew each other well, but Kerry was Sonja's best friend and what Matt had just done to her was pretty mean.

Sonja was about to make him pay for his big mouth.

CHAPTER 2

• •

TRUTH, DARE... OR LIE?

"Truth or dare, Matt?" cooed Sonja. She was sitting cross-legged on the grass, a tanned picture of glowing health in white shorts and a skimpy, strappy top.

"I'll take a dare, please, Son."

She smiled sweetly at Matt, knowing exactly how to knock the smirk off his face.

"I dare you to take your father's beloved Mercedes SLK sports car – which, for anyone who doesn't know, is worth the price of a small house – from the garage, drive it round town, park it on double yellow lines and leave it there."

Matt was aghast. "No way, Son!"

"Uh-oh, wrong answer," Sonja tutted. "That means you have to do a forfeit."

"Oh come *on*, Sonja. You know that's a non-starter!" wailed Matt. "Dad would kill me if he knew I'd even touched his wretched car, let alone driven the thing. You're being unfair."

"Sorry, mate," Ollie chipped in, laughing, "but life's not fair, is it?"

Matt looked crestfallen. He was perfectly aware that this was Sonja's revenge for his being so cruel to Kerry and he sorely wished he'd kept his mouth shut. Not that he'd admit it to anyone.

"Is that a refusal then, Matt?" asked Sonja sweetly.

Matt nodded glumly.

"Right then. For a forfeit I want you to spend the next two turns standing over there by that bush."

"Easy," Matt smirked as he leapt to his feet. "Cheers, Son!"

"Oh! Something I forgot to mention," Sonja continued. "I *do* want you standing, but on your *head*. With an apple in your mouth."

Everyone roared with laughter as Matt stood, open-mouthed and horrified. The gang howled even louder when he dutifully carried out the task, with his face gradually turning a deeper shade of purple and dribbling profusely from his open mouth where the apple was neatly wedged. It was a bit of a comedown for someone who spent his life trying to be the coolest person on the planet.

Then it was Joe Gladwin's turn to spin the bottle. When it came to rest in front of Sonja she immediately chose a truth – and Joe's mind went blank. It couldn't have stopped at anyone worse. She was beautiful and witty, and frightened him half to death.

He racked his brains frantically for something interesting and/or amusing to ask her, but came up with a big, fat nothing.

"Uhhh... umm..." he muttered under his breath.

"Come on," heckled Sonja. "Don't keep me in suspense, Joe. Hurry up!"

Joe felt his face turn red and begin to throb with embarrassment. He cursed the fact that he blushed so easily and wished he'd stayed at home playing computer games rather than put himself through this torture.

He felt as if everyone's eyes were boring into him, staring at him, waiting for him to say something funny. He felt under pressure to join in, perform, be one of the gang, when in fact he felt really uneasy sitting there.

"Umm... is it true that you fancy Matt?" he eventually blurted out, which was the first thing that came into his head.

Several groans were heard. Everyone in the world knew that Sonja didn't fancy Matt.

"Um *no*, Joe, it isn't." Sonja replied, her voice full of sarcasm. "It's you I really fancy. Didn't you know?"

She laughed and Joe looked down at the ground with a face the colour of fuchsia, his humiliation complete. Like everyone else, he knew she was joking. A drop-dead stunning girl like Sonja would never fancy a scruffy little runt like him.

Sensing how uncomfortable Joe must be feeling, Kerry made a great show of picking up the bottle.

"OK, my turn," she called, spinning it round. When it stopped at Catrina and she chose a dare, Kerry challenged her to take her bra off under her low-cut top without showing her chest to anyone. This rapidly diverted attention from Joe's duff question and gave everyone a good giggle as Cat attempted the near impossible deed.

Catrina relished the chance to be the centre of attention and wasn't at all embarrassed by the challenge. Belting out the tune to *The Stripper*, she unhooked the back of her bra and began wriggling out of it. Only when one of her ample boobs threatened to pop out did she give a girlish squeal of fake coyness.

In less than thirty seconds she had deftly removed the black, lacy, D-cup number which she then held proudly aloft for everyone to see.

"Waa-haaay!" Matt hollered from the bush, spitting out the apple that had been threatening to choke him and falling on to his knees in a heap. "You could hold a party in that bra! Can I have a closer look?"

Attempting to stand up caused a sudden rush of blood to Matt's head so instead he crawled back to the group on his hands and knees, grinning and leching at the same time.

Cat wasn't impressed. She and Matt had gone out together for a short time recently, but the affair had ended abruptly when she saw Matt getting off with Ollie's twin sister, Natasha. Although the pair were now officially on friendly terms, Catrina was still a little miffed that he had humiliated her so publicly.

"Get lost, creep," she snarled. "This is one bra you'll never get your hands on again."

"Ooh, touchy!" Matt laughed, pleased that he'd got the intended reaction. Although he sometimes felt twinges of remorse at the way he'd treated Cat, he still found it impossible to miss an opportunity to make her mad. She was so easy to wind up.

Now it was Catrina's turn to devise the line of questioning. She was delighted when the bottle pointed at Joe. Like a cat about to pounce on a defenceless mouse, she knew she would have fun playing with him.

"OK, Joe, truth or dare?" Cat demanded, her grey eyes glinting merrily.

Joe's heart sank for a second time. He really loathed this game. It didn't suit his sensitive nature at all. He didn't even know what he was still doing here – he should have left ages ago.

He wished he'd gone before everyone started this stupid charade, but he'd come with Ollie and thought it would have looked odd if he'd left on his own. And, of course, Ollie was having the time of his life, so Joe hadn't wanted to be a killjoy by suggesting they leave. Now, with the prospect of Cat the man-eater about to maul him, he sorely wished he had.

"Um, I guess it'll have to be a truth," Joe said weakly.

Cat pondered over her question. Other than the fact that they had a crossover of friends, she and Joe didn't really connect at any level. Cat didn't know much about him and, as far as she was concerned, Joe was shy, awkward and a bit of a geek. Totally different to her. Catrina oozed confidence from every pore.

She wondered if there was anything more to him than the studious, good-guy impression he gave out. Were there any hidden depths?

Perhaps he was a secret tattoo-freak, or a hardened

criminal with a police record. It wouldn't surprise Cat at all to find out that he had another life, one that he kept secret from the rest of the world.

"You've got the reputation for being a bit of a goody two shoes," she announced. "So what I want to know from you, Joe, is whether you've ever done anything risqué in your life. Like handed your homework in late, or stolen sweeties from the corner shop, or got hammered on your mum's Baileys..."

She paused as inspiration suddenly hit her. "Yes, that's it!" she shrieked, laughing. " I know what I can ask you, Joe. Have you, our resident Mr Perfect, ever been so drunk you didn't know what you were doing?"

Catrina's eyebrows were raised and her eyes bulged as she giggled wickedly at such a ridiculous notion. So did everyone else.

Joe remained stony-faced at the question, wondering whether to tell the truth. He knew it would be a real shocker if he did. After a few seconds of mulling it over, he gave his answer.

"Er, no. No, I haven't," he replied quietly.

Only Joe knew that he was lying.

CHAPTER 3

●●●●●●●●●●●●●●●●●●●●●●●●●●●●

THE POST-MORTEM

It was way past midnight when everyone finally
decided to go home. After leaving Cat at the end
of her road, the others turned into the high street,
which was brightly lit but almost deserted.

"So, do you think Catrina was expecting you
to pick *her* when she dared you to kiss the most
fanciable girl at the barbie?" Sonja asked Ollie.

Always very sceptical about her cousin's
motives, Sonja had immediately been suspicious
of Cat's dare. Ollie and Catrina had gone out
together briefly after Matt had dumped her: now
that they were 'just good friends', Sonja could
imagine her trying to pull off a trick like that.

The way she saw it, if Catrina had been picked
out as more attractive than anyone else –
especially Sonja – it would bolster her ego

hugely *and* be one in the eye for her cousin.

"Oh, I dunno," Ollie replied, contorting his face as if he'd been sucking a bag of lemons. "I'm not sure she's *that* calculating. Anyway, I couldn't have snogged her. Not now. She'd eat me for breakfast and still have room for Joe, wouldn't she, Joey?"

Ollie looked back to where Joe was loitering behind them, slouching along in a world of his own. He was staring at the pavement as he walked just behind Kerry, hands deep in his pockets, brain deeper in thought. He wasn't even bothering to try and engage her in any kind of conversation.

Typical, thought Ollie. *Useless at talking to girls – always has been, always will be.*

Joe was Ollie's closest friend and someone he held in high regard, but it didn't stop him being exasperated at times by Joe's excruciating shyness with the opposite sex. And the fact that he often seemed totally incapable of communicating with anyone other than Ollie niggled him even more.

"Oi, Joey, are you listening?" Ollie hollered.

Joe's head shot up and, with a startled look on his face, he grunted a "Huh, what?" back.

Ollie raised his eyebrows and motioned frantically at Joe to talk to Kerry, who had stopped to look in a shop window. Joe gave his friend a weak smile in return and, shrugging his shoulders, went back to studying the ground in front of him.

The truth was he didn't have a clue what to say to Kerry or most other people for that matter (but Kerry in particular). The fact that Joe fancied her like mad didn't help – it just made him even more nervous. And anyway, at the moment, making conversation was the last thing on his mind.

Joe was worrying about Cat's question at the barbie earlier. He wondered if it had been meant as a joke, which was how it had seemed, or if she actually *knew* something.

Realistically, he doubted it. After all, it wasn't even as though he was a hardened drinker – he'd just had the odd binge or two every now and again when life got on top of him. But it wasn't something he felt he could confess to the others, and he never got drunk in front of them. He couldn't bear the thought of everyone scrutinising his motives.

Joe had been so relieved when the barbie had come to an end. He hadn't enjoyed it one bit – what with that dumb spin the bottle game and the fact that he'd been within spitting distance of Kerry all evening, yet had hardly said three words to her. The whole thing had been a total disaster.

Joe watched Kerry as she walked slightly ahead

of him. She was wearing her red-brown curly hair pulled back into a ponytail so that a mass of curls bobbed about at the back of her head with each step. Joe caught a glimpse of her bare neck and sighed deeply. He imagined burying his head into her hair, neck and shoulders, kissing her passionately...

As if aware that she was being stared at, Kerry turned round and peered at Joe. Looking quickly away, he blushed furiously and prayed that she couldn't read his mind.

Kerry smiled a little uneasily. She knew Joe was shy and she felt a bit sorry for him.

"It's getting a bit chilly now, isn't it?" she said, trying to get a conversation going. Talking about the weather was as lame an opener as any she'd ever tried, but it was all she could think of.

"Mmmm." Joe glanced up at her for a millisecond before looking away again. What else could he *say*?

"Did you have a good time tonight?" Kerry asked, smiling.

"It was OK, I s'pose..."

Joe searched every corner of his mind, frantically trying to think of something else to add, something that would engage Kerry and keep them talking for hours. But he couldn't think of anything.

So he kept quiet, mentally tearing into himself for being so inept, so withdrawn, so useless!

Kerry was beginning to wish she'd kept her mouth shut. Joe was a nice guy, but he was never going to set the world alight with his sparkling wit and stimulating small talk. Maybe he channelled all his energy into his school work? Kerry knew he was a bit of a boffin because he was in the top stream of all his classes.

Perhaps she ought to talk to him about schoolwork or something. *God!* she thought. *How boring would that be?*

They carried on in silence.

● ● ●

The boys walked through the town centre with Kerry and Sonja, then peeled back to their own homes. The girls carried on walking, enjoying the cool air and quiet stillness all around them. They were making their way to Sonja's, where Kerry was staying the night.

"That wasn't a bad evening for a spur of the moment thing, was it?" said Sonja.

"It was *OK*," Kerry replied less certainly "I mean, it would have been better if Mick had been there."

She sighed dramatically. Kerry had had the

hots for Mick ever since he joined The Loud, Ollie and Joe's band. She'd been trying to engage him in some kind of conversation for ages, but he hadn't taken the hint.

Sonja had always been encouraging, giving Kerry tips on how to get herself noticed, but even she now thought that Mick wasn't interested.

"Yeah, I'm beginning to think you're on to a loser there, Kez. I hate to tell you this, but I saw him with someone when I was in town earlier today."

"What? Who?" Kerry wailed, crestfallen.

"I dunno who she was. She looked like a bit of a bimbo to me. You know, big hair and too much make-up. Like a giant Barbie doll really."

"I always hated my Barbie doll," Kerry said through gritted teeth. "I ripped her head off and burnt it when I was seven. So why didn't you tell me before?"

"I've been waiting for the right moment. I didn't want to tell you earlier 'cause I knew it would put a downer on your evening."

"I s'pose so. Oh well, there goes another one, I guess."

"Plenty more fish in the sea, I say." Sonja said cheerfully.

"Yeah, it's just that I'm swimming in the wrong waters," Kerry muttered. "And while I'm on a downer, I could've killed Matt tonight. I *wish* we didn't always have to end up playing those stupid games. They're so humiliating. I couldn't *believe* it when he started going on about my chest!"

"I *know*," said Sonja sympathetically as she recalled the scene. "It was pretty rotten of him to get so personal. I was surprised. I know he can be insensitive, but I didn't think he'd go that far. Maybe he genuinely didn't realise you had a thing about your... erm... boob size."

"Possibly," Kerry said, unconvinced. "I thought perhaps he was trying to look cool in front of his mates. You know, humiliate a girl just to get a laugh. But thanks for sticking up for me and getting back at him. I really appreciate it."

"No worries. Though I do think you're far too nice sometimes. You ought to give as good as you get a bit more."

"I know."

Kerry felt like a little kid being told off by her mum for not standing up to the school bully. Sonja was good at making her feel inadequate. Kerry was sure it wasn't deliberate – it was just something in Sonja's personality.

As the relationship between the two friends had developed over the years, Kerry had realised that they were total opposites in virtually every way. Sonja could be a bit of a bossy-boots, domineering and loud, and relishing being the centre of attention.

Kerry was much quieter, more sensible, definitely not a limelight hogger, and mostly happy for Sonja to tell her what to do. And yet they clicked, they were best friends and had been since junior school. Strange really.

Kerry felt proud that someone as popular, stunning-looking and ambitious as Sonja would give her the time of day, let alone be her only real confidante. A lot of girls were desperate to hang out with Sonja, but she'd chosen Kerry and only Kerry. No other girl shared the same level of intimacy. It made Kerry feel good.

Sonja's house was one of those detached, four-bedroom executive homes in a quiet cul-de-sac on a smart estate. Kerry loved going there. It was so different to the boring 1930s semi she and her family lived in.

Although her house was only a few streets away, it was a world apart from *this*. As well as her own very spacious bedroom, Sonja even had a personal phone extension. And the Harveys had a cappuccino maker in the kitchen, satellite TV and Surround Sound, plus a lot more things that Kerry would love to have but knew her family could never afford.

Sonja went up to the front door and slipped her key in the lock.

As quietly as they could, the pair tiptoed into the house and headed for the kitchen. It was 1.30 in the morning and while Sonja knew her parents were usually pretty relaxed about her social life, she did worry about accidentally waking anyone up at such a late hour.

Switching the kettle on, Sonja began rummaging in the kitchen cupboards for biscuits while Kerry slumped in a chair and kicked off her too-tight shoes.

"I'm whacked," she said. "That was a mammoth walk home. Next time remind me to book a taxi."

"Oh, you old misery guts," Sonja chided jokingly, "it was fun. I love walking through town late at night. And we had the guys with us for most of the way, so it wasn't as if it was unsafe or anything."

"I know."

"Joe can be a weird one at times though, can't he?" Sonja continued. "He hardly said a word at Matt's and even less on the way home."

"He's just shy. Not everyone in the world is as loud as you, you know," said Kerry. "There's got to be room for quiet people as well – people who do the listening rather than the talking."

"But he doesn't do either! He's on Planet Joe most of the time. He looked pretty fazed when Catty Cat asked him about his drinking, though. You don't think he's a secret alky, do you?"

Kerry shook her head. "He's the last person you'd expect to be knocking back bottles of gin. He's far too sensible."

"Yeah, s'pose so," Sonja agreed, frowning. "You know, I *hate* sensible people, they're so... so boring!"

Sonja waved her hand dramatically in front of her and Kerry giggled. It was such a sweeping statement and so typical of Sonja, who lacked tolerance at the best of times.

"Your coffee's ready," Sonja carried on, oblivious to her friend's stifled chuckles. "Shall we have it in my room?"

Without waiting for a reply, she made her way towards the staircase. Kerry followed dutifully and the girls crept up to Sonja's room where her mother had already made up the guest bed for Kerry.

Crawling under their duvets, the girls spent ages whispering and giggling together about anything that happened to pop into their minds. Actually, if Kerry was honest, it was Sonja who did most of the talking. Kerry just grunted occasionally while her friend rattled on.

It was after four in the morning before Sonja realised that Kerry hadn't spoken for absolutely ages. She was, in fact, asleep.

CHAPTER 4

● ●

CAT AND MOUSE

Kerry woke with a start. She was in a strange bed and for a few moments she didn't have a clue where she was. Then she heard a rasping sound to her left that she gradually recognised as snoring.

Turning her head, she saw Sonja sleeping soundly in the bed next to her.

Kerry craned her neck to see the clock on Sonja's bedside table. It was eleven thirty. She was late.

Panic-stricken, she leapt out of bed. She had told her parents she wouldn't be home any later than midday as the family were going to see one of her aunts for Sunday tea.

It was a once-a-year visit and although Valerie was by far her favourite aunt, at sixteen years of age Kerry figured her time could be better spent in her room listening to CDs rather than catching up on family news with distant relations.

However, against her better judgement, she had reluctantly agreed to go. It was a long drive and her dad would be livid if she held them up.

Clutching the duvet around her with one hand, and carrying her toothbrush and hairbrush in the other, Kerry opened the bedroom door and looked from left to right. The last thing she needed right now was to have to make polite conversation with Sonja's parents, or even her sisters or brother.

She could hear 'family noises' downstairs, but the coast was clear and she scurried across the landing to the plush bathroom opposite.

Kerry gave her face a quick splash with water, brushed her teeth and hair, went to the loo and scuttled back to Sonja's room where she hurriedly got dressed.

Then she went over to Sonja and began prodding her awake.

"Son. Sonja! I have to go. *Son!*"

Sonja stopped snoring, turned over and peered at her friend through mascara-smudged eyes.

"Wh-what? What's happened?"

"I'm going. I have to go to my aunt's this afternoon. I told you yesterday."

"So? Why did you wake me up to tell me again?" Sonja demanded grumpily. She wasn't at her best first thing in the morning (even though it was now nearly noon).

"I'm just telling you, OK? And thanks for putting me up."

Kerry quickly gathered her stuff together and made for the bedroom door.

Sonja muttered something completely unintelligible, then rolled on to her front again, no doubt for another few hours' kip.

• • •

"I'm not surprised Kerry found a shop window more interesting than you! You hardly said a word to her all the way home."

Ollie was standing behind the counter of the End-of-the-Line café where he worked, wielding a dishcloth. Joe had popped in to say hello and Ollie was taking the opportunity to try and find out why his friend had been even quieter than usual the night before.

Rather than take him to task at the time, Ollie had waited until today to mention it – and in a very jokey manner.

"I mean," he continued, grinning, "you had a perfect opportunity to have a conversation with a girl there – even if it *was* only Kerry – and you blew it, mate!"

Joe gave a little smile. Not even Ollie knew that Joe fancied Kerry. "Yeah, I know. I was pretty crap, wasn't I? But then my mind just goes completely blank, you know? Girls – it's like they're from another planet. I just don't *get* them."

"I've noticed," Ollie laughed. "But you've just got to be yourself, talk to them like you talk to me. Act natural."

"I know, I know, but that's easy for you to say. Girls *like* you."

Ollie hooted with laughter. "They like *you*, too. It's not as though you smell or anything. You've just got to give them a chance."

"But they don't give *me* a chance. They look at me with pity or disgust, or they don't even notice me at all. It's not as though I look like Leonardo DiCaprio, is it?" Joe stared forlornly into his Coke.

"C'mon, mate," said Ollie encouragingly, "you're doing yourself down! *You're* not Quasimodo either."

"Sometimes I feel like Quasimodo..."

"And that's half your problem, you pillock! Your lack of confidence comes over within seconds of a girl meeting you. You *assume* they don't like you and that puts them off straight away. Instead of always being negative about yourself, you need to concentrate on the positive."

"Which is what, exactly?"

"Oh for God's sake, man, don't you know?"

"Er, no. I didn't realise there was anything good about me whatsoever."

Ollie ran his fingers through his hair in exasperation.

"You've got loads going for you. I can't believe you don't see it! You're super-intelligent, you've got a huge future waiting for you, whatever you do. You're a really great person, you're funny, good-looking in an indie band drummer sort of way... need I go on?"

Seeing Joe's worried expression, Ollie gave his friend a reassuring grin.

"You just have to relax and enjoy life a bit more. The more uptight you are, the more it puts girls off. Look, you can practise on Natasha – she's coming home for a few days soon. I can set you up, if you like?"

"Yeah, sure," Joe shot back. "Like *she's* going to be interested in *me*."

"She would – she's easy. Honest, she'd be asking *you* out." Ollie chuckled wickedly.

Joe had to laugh. He knew Ollie was joking. His twin sister Natasha, who was a model working in London, spent her whole life mixing with beautiful people. The chances of her even noticing Joe were zilch.

"It'd be great to turn her down though, wouldn't it?" Joe said, warming to the idea. "Winstead's answer to Kate Moss asks me for a date and I say 'sorry, I'm washing my hair'."

The boys' laughter was interrupted by a voice from the kitchen.

"Come on, Ollie, I'm paying you to work here, not chat."

Ollie's Uncle Nick, who owned the café, was obviously getting a bit miffed by the fact that Ollie sounded as if he was having a good time rather than cleaning tables.

Raising his eyebrows in mock surprise, Ollie gave Joe a meaningful look. "On my way," he called back.

"I'll leave you to it, then. I'm off home now," Joe smiled.

"Yeah," said Ollie. "Catch you later."

Joe walked out of the café into bright sunshine and turned right. Then, feeling the warm sun on his face, he made a snap decision to go home via the scenic route, through the park, and began sauntering in the opposite direction.

It was a fab day again, warm and sunny without being too humid. Joe now felt in a much better mood – no, a *really* good mood – after the praise that Ollie had dished out.

It was just the sort of day for sitting on the grass, watching the world go by, maybe doing a bit of writing.

Ollie was the only person in the world who knew that Joe wrote songs – and he had been sworn to secrecy.

Joe wasn't embarrassed by the fact that he preferred putting his emotions down on paper rather than voicing them out loud, but he was afraid that people might take the mickey out of him for doing it. Being hugely sensitive, he just couldn't take such flak. Even Ollie realised that.

Joe patted the back pocket of his jeans and felt the hard-edged outline of the little notebook and pencil he always kept there. Whenever inspiration took him (and he was alone) he would take the pad out, open it at a crisply clean, blank page and scribble down a few words, maybe a line or two of a song or a phrase he liked the sound of. Anything that popped into his head really.

This afternoon felt like a good time to write.

Joe walked through the park until he found his favourite spot. It was under the boughs of a huge old oak tree whose roots fanned out into splendid v-shapes before gradually tapering into the ground. Joe could sit in the middle of this gnarled formation, between two of the roots, and feel as if he was sitting in a big wooden armchair.

From there, he could look out on the most wonderful view of the lake with its mix of wildlife, boats for hire and the kiosk that sold ice-creams and teas.

It was a brilliant place to be creative.

Joe took the notepad from his pocket and sat down. He began scribbling, inspiration flowing through him.

Totally engrossed in his writing, he didn't notice a figure walking purposefully towards him until he heard the *clop clop clop* of heels on the concrete path. By the time he realised someone was coming, it was too late.

"Well, if it isn't Mr Goody Two Shoes!"

Joe's head shot up at the sound of Cat's rasping voice and he felt his stomach tighten. Although Cat was one of the gang and they were supposed to be friends, Joe never really felt comfortable with her. He was terrified of the bitchy comments she was always coming out with and her in-your-face sexuality.

"What are you up to?" she demanded, peering at him under the shady tree.

Joe didn't answer. As usual, his mind had completely disengaged from his brain and he was suddenly very aware of the incriminating notebook and pencil in his hands.

Cat moved a little closer and Joe could make out the glint in her eye and the sneer on her face.

"You're not doing *homework*, are you?"

Joe looked at her mutely.

"You *are*, aren't you?" said Catrina incredulously.

"It's the weekend, it's a nice summer's day and you're sitting here swotting. I can hardly believe it!"

Joe flushed with embarrassment. It didn't matter that what Cat was saying wasn't true. The fact that she thought it was enough to humiliate him.

Catrina waited for Joe to speak, but he could find nothing to say. It seemed to Cat that Joe was ignoring her and she hated being ignored.

"I mean, I know you haven't got a life, Joe, but I thought even you might have something better to do on a Sunday afternoon," she pouted. "Like going train-spotting. Or browsing through your stamp collection."

Joe carried on staring at her, speechless. He couldn't understand why she was being such a cow, but felt powerless to stop her. He wished she would just leave him alone, but to his horror, she came even closer.

Cat knelt down and put her face so close to Joe's that he could feel her breath. Her eyes goggled madly and her lipsticked mouth opened and closed rapidly as she babbled on.

Joe could no longer understand what she was saying. He imagined himself putting his hands round her throat and strangling her until she couldn't speak. If only he had the guts...

He didn't, of course. Instead, he just got redder and more flustered and worried by what she might say or do next.

Suddenly, Catrina made a grab for Joe's notebook to get a closer look. This immediately sent Joe's stomach into even tighter knots of panic. There was no way he could let Catrina know what he was really up to. Once she'd got over the fit of hysterical laughter it would send her into, she would rush off to tell the rest of the crowd.

In the space of a millisecond Joe had snapped the book shut and sat on it.

This was exactly the sort of messing around Catrina loved, even if it was only with Joe who was, to her mind, possibly the least fanciable male in the universe. She gave a little shriek and lunged at Joe, who started backwards to avoid her and cracked his head on the tree trunk.

"Ouch!" Joe put his hand to the back of his head and accidentally clipped Catrina on the chin.

He was mortified.

"Uh, sorry!" he said, aghast. Catrina smiled wickedly. She didn't seem to mind at all. If anything, it made her all the more zealous in her attempts to get at his notepad.

"You are mean, Joey," she giggled. "I only want to have a little peek. *Pleeeeease!*"

She looked imploringly at Joe, pouting her lips and pleading with her eyes, just like a child who was desperate to get its own way. Her hands were grabbing at his thighs, trying to push them out of the way so that she could get hold of the notebook.

To Cat this was all a big game; to Joe it was possibly the most cringeworthy moment of his life so far. To have this overbearing female pawing at him and, more importantly, intent on exposing his secret passion was just *unbearable*.

Catrina suddenly lost all patience and decided she'd had enough. As she'd always suspected, Joe was no fun at all.

Dropping the playful charade, she jumped up and adopted a more condescending tone.

"God, Joe, you're so boring! For the life of me I can't understand what Ollie and the rest of them see in you. You've got to be the dullest, most fun-free person I've *ever* met. You've got nothing to say for yourself, your dress sense is appalling and your hair's a mess. All you ever do is swot and simper and skulk about in the background. *Boring*."

Not waiting to see the effect of her words, Cat turned and flounced off up the footpath.

Completely crushed, Joe ripped the page from his notepad, screwed it into a ball and threw it on the ground.

Sod you, he thought. *Sod you all!*

CHAPTER 5

• •

SONJA GETS STOOD UP

Anna Michaels, waitress at the End-of-the-Line café, shut the door of the drinks fridge and turned around. She smiled sympathetically at Sonja, who was standing at the counter drumming her cerise-painted fingernails irritably on the stainless steel worktop.

"Still no sign, then?"

"No," huffed Sonja. "I should have known he'd be late – he always is. If he's not here soon, we'll miss the start of the film."

Anna waved the coffee jug at Sonja.

"Top up?"

Sonja nodded and muttered "Thanks" before returning to her seat in the big bay window. She was beginning to get really annoyed. What the heck did Matt think he was playing at? He should have arrived twenty minutes ago and she was getting seriously sick of waiting.

She wished Kerry had been able to come instead, as she wasn't convinced Matt would remember to turn up at all.

Sonja secretly cursed Kerry's six-year-old brother, Lewis, who needed babysitting while Kerry's parents went out for the evening. If it wasn't for him, she and Kez would be guzzling Diet Coke and scoffing huge boxes of popcorn by now. Instead, she was sitting in the café wondering whether she'd been stood up.

She was jolted back to reality by the *ping!* of the café door being opened. About time too! Sonja grabbed her bag and leapt up from her seat.

"Don't you dare sit down!" she snapped. "If we don't go now, we might as well not bother."

Turning around with a deliberately furrowed brow and a miserable pout, Sonja walked right into... Natasha Stanton.

"Oh!"

Ollie's twin sister was the last person Sonja had expected to see. She had heard that Natasha was coming back home for a day or so, but she'd forgotten when and certainly hadn't expected her to come into the café.

Sonja always imagined that now Natasha was a successful model living it up in London,

Winstead would seem small-town and insignificant. Quite what she was doing slumming it in a grotty backstreet café – as Sonja figured she'd see it – God only knew!

"Hello, Sonja, how are you?" Natasha beamed a big, perfect, pearly-white smile in Sonja's direction.

"Uh, fine, thanks."

"I'm looking for Ollie. You haven't seen him, have you? Mum thought he might be working in here tonight."

"No, he's next door in the record shop," Sonja replied. "Stocktaking with Nick. Er, sorry about the yelling, I thought you were Matt. We're supposed to be going to the pictures tonight."

Natasha's eyes widened. "You're not dating *him* are you?" she said incredulously.

"No way!" Sonja laughed. "Give me some credit, please. No, we were both at a loose end, or at least I thought we were. Matt's obviously had a better offer."

"I didn't *think* you were crazy enough to go out with him. I always credited you with more sense. And taste."

"Hang on," Sonja grinned, "that doesn't say much for you, does it? It wasn't so long ago that you and Matt had a bit of a thing going, if I remember rightly."

"Yeah, but I've always had abysmal taste in guys. It's a known fact. Anyway, I was only doing him a favour by saving him from Catrina Osgood."

Sonja sniggered. She was beginning to really like Natasha. Mind you, Sonja would warm to anyone who was disparaging about her cousin. The fact that Natasha had, albeit unwittingly, caused Matt and Catrina to split up did raise her in Sonja's estimation.

Sonja had never particularly warmed to Natasha when she lived in Winstead. Natasha had always seemed so hugely sophisticated – stuck-up, even – and much older than everyone else in her year at school.

And Sonja had been dead jealous when she'd heard that Natasha had been scouted by a London model agency and offered a contract, a flat and a much more glamorous life than anyone living in Winstead could ever imagine.

On the odd occasion that Natasha came home to visit her family, Sonja tended to give her a wide berth. If she was being honest, it was because she couldn't stand the competition as much as anything else.

Sonja liked the fact that she turned heads wherever she went. With her honey-blonde hair (natural, not dyed), tanned skin and cornflower blue eyes, she knew she stood out in a roomful of people.

Unless Natasha was around. Sonja had always done her best to avoid playing second fiddle to 'the model from London'.

Natasha walked round to the big table where Sonja was sitting. "I think I'll get a coffee while I'm here. D'you fancy one?"

"No thanks, I'm OK. Come and join me though when you've got it."

Natasha nodded, smiling. She walked, no *sashayed* (like models do) up to Anna at the counter and put in her order. Then she came back to where Sonja was sitting, slid on to the red leatherette seat opposite her, pulled out a packet of cigarettes and offered one to Sonja.

"No thanks, I don't," Sonja said, wrinkling her nose with distaste.

"I wish I didn't. Costs me a fortune." She took a long drag, then exhaled a puff of smoke up towards the ceiling. "Plays havoc with my skin too."

"God, really?" Sonja took a look at the immaculately made-up face across the table. "But you always look so good."

Natasha shook her head. "You should see me when I'm slobbing out at home on a day off. No make-up, ratty old dressing gown, gob full of pizza—"

"Pizza!" exclaimed Sonja. "I thought all you models lived on lettuce leaves and fresh air."

"Yeah, well, some do." Natasha pulled a face. "I couldn't. Mind you, I sometimes wish I could just sit down and eat a home-cooked, well balanced meal and have time to enjoy it. Most of the time I have to eat and run – y'know? A burger here, choccy bar there."

Sonja was intrigued. "So, what's a typical day like when you're working?"

"Hmmm, depends really. Most of the time is spent waiting for my booker to ring—"

"Booker?"

"The girl at the agency who gets me all my work. So I might get up at ten, call the agency to see what – if anything – is going on. Sometimes I've got time to watch *This Morning* while I'm getting ready to go out, but often I have to bolt my breakfast and get dressed all at the same time."

"Then I suppose you have a hard morning's posing till lunch?"

"No way! Lunch is usually a Coke and a Mars bar on the hoof. That's why it's so hard to keep fit and healthy – you can never be sure how your day is going to be structured."

Natasha looked at Sonja's horrified face through a haze of smoke. "Then in the afternoon

I might have a load of go-sees to endure, which is where I traipse around magazines and advertising agencies showing them my book."

"What's that?"

"It's kind of like a portfolio of the best pictures photographers have taken of me. I put them together in a book to show fashion editors and such like."

"Oh. *That* sounds exciting," Sonja said, picturing herself nosing around swanky magazine publishers, maybe bumping into the odd celebrity or two. Natasha soon brought her back to earth.

"God, you must be joking!" she grimaced. "It's got to be the most demoralising part of the job. You get called to a casting for, say, a magazine shoot. You go along and find that there are thirty other models there, so you mill about in a grotty corridor for ages waiting to be called. Then, when you finally get to see the fashion editor, they flick through your book for about ten seconds, say 'thanks' – and that's it. An hour's walk from your flat, a thirty-minute wait in a corridor, fifteen seconds of glory and then you find out the next day someone else got the job."

"Oh." Sonja was disappointed. "So it's not all it's cracked up to be then?" she ventured.

"Don't get me wrong," Natasha replied, an earnest look on her face. "You do get to go to some good parties. And you often walk away from jobs with freebies. It's just that the good stuff is only one per cent of the job – the rest is pretty boring really."

"Yeah, but I bet it beats packing boxes in a factory though, doesn't it?"

Natasha's face broke into a huge grin. "Funnily enough, yes. God, I must sound like a right old moaner! Of course there are good things too, like putting on incredibly expensive clothes, and travelling abroad. So I'm not complaining. Not really. I'm just telling you like it is, y'know, in case you were interested in doing it yourself."

Sonja's self-esteem was immediately boosted by the compliment and Natasha soared even further in her estimation. She loved it when people massaged her ego – it always left her wanting more.

"Uh, I don't think I could be a model," she continued, fishing for compliments. "I mean, I'm not nearly good-looking enough."

"Sonja, you *are*. You could do it. I meet loads of girls who are models and they aren't nearly as stunning as you. And I bet you're naturally skinny, too."

"Well, I never seem to put on weight, even though I do eat a lot of junk food."

"There you go then. You've got looks, stamina

– and now you've got a contact too. Seriously, if you're ever interested in giving it a go, boring though it can be, let me know and I'll put you in touch with a few people."

"Wow, thanks," Sonja gushed. "I'll bear it in mind. I mean, really I'd like to get into public relations – that's my big dream. But, well, who knows what'll happen in the next couple of years? I might flunk my exams..."

"In which case modelling could be something to fall back on. Plus it would be a good way to find out about PR, especially with advertising work."

"Mmm. It's certainly worth thinking about," Sonja nodded thoughtfully. "How long are you here?"

"I go back next Thursday. Why?"

"Well me and Kerry are going clubbing tomorrow night. If you're not doing anything, why don't you come along?"

"Great! I'd love to," grinned Natasha. "Kerry won't mind if I butt in?"

"No, course not. It'll be great – we'll have a right laugh. D'you want another coffee?"

"Please."

Sonja stood up and went over to where Anna was polishing the ancient coffee machine. As she got to the counter, the phone rang. Anna gave

Sonja an apologetic look as she answered the call.

"It's for you," she said and then whispered, "sounds like Matt."

Sonja pulled a face as she grabbed the phone from Anna's outstretched hand. She glanced at the clock on the wall – 7.45 pm. What sort of time did he call this? Sonja relished the thought of tearing into Matt in front of Natasha and Anna. She wouldn't let him make a fool of her.

"Yes?" The tone was distinctly cold.

"Son, hi. It's Matt."

"Matt?" she squawked back. "Matt who? I don't think I know anyone called that. I used to have a friend called Matt but I dumped him because he was an unreliable sod."

"Sonja, listen, this is serious. I was on my way to you, but I didn't get as far as the café because I found Joe in the road."

Sonja dropped the haughty tone to one of concerned surprise. "What do you mean, in the road? What, like run over?"

"No, just completely out of it. You know, like virtually comatose. He was slumped against a lamp-post on Rosermann Street. Totally gone. Drunk. Absolutely off his face."

CHAPTER 6

● ●

HUNG-OVER... AND HUNG UP

"No, really? Joey Gladwin? I can hardly believe it!"

Kerry's eyes were like saucers as she listened to Sonja relaying the story. Kerry was the third person Sonja had told after she'd got off the phone to Matt. Anna and Natasha had listened incredulously as Sonja had given them an abbreviated version of events before picking up the café phone and calling Kerry.

"I know! Talk about the person least likely to. I didn't think he even drank. But Matt said he could hardly open his eyes, let alone speak. He didn't dare take him home – you know what his mum's like..."

Kerry couldn't help nodding, even though Sonja couldn't see her. They all knew how over-protective Joe's mum was.

"...So Matt shovelled him into his car and took him back to his house," continued Sonja. "Apparently, he sat Joe in the garden and put the hose on him to sober him up! And when he did come round, he threw up all over Matt's black leather jacket – you know, his favourite? The one from Italy that he's always going on about. Matt was speechless! You can just imagine it, can't you? Anyway, that's when Matt rang me."

Kerry was worried, unable to rationalise Joe's strange and uncharacteristic behaviour. "So what *had* happened?" she quizzed. "Why was he drunk?"

"Matt still doesn't know. Joe was pretty incoherent."

"Has anyone tried to get in touch with Ollie? Maybe he was out with Joe. He might be worried about him."

"Uh, no," Sonja countered. "Ollie can't have been involved. He's working next door. Has been all day. But Tasha and me will go and see him as soon as I get off the phone."

"Tasha? What, Ollie's sister? What's she doing there?"

"She's on a break from London. She came in looking for Ollie while I was waiting for Matt. We've been sat here gossiping for ages."

Kerry felt a pang of jealousy. She pictured

Sonja and Natasha having a great time in the café, while she was stuck at home looking after her wretched little brother. She felt strangely threatened by Natasha, though she didn't know why. There certainly wasn't any logical reason why she should feel that way. But she did.

Stupid really. She tried to push the negative thoughts to the back of her mind and carried on with a forced lightness to her voice.

"Oh, right. Lovely. So what have you been chatting about?"

"Modelling. Guys. You know, the usual stuff. I've invited her to come out with us tomorrow night. That'll be cool, won't it?"

It most certainly will not *be cool*, Kerry thought, as feelings of insecurity and resentment surged up. Why did Sonja suddenly want to go around with someone who's only in town once in a blue moon? And someone she'd never had much to do with for all those years when Natasha *did* live at home? Why the sudden *girlfriends* act?

Kerry realised she was as jealous as hell, but she didn't have the guts to say anything about it.

"Yeah, sure, that'd be great," she lied. "Anyway, I must go, I can hear Lewis messing about upstairs. I'll see you tomorrow. But ring me if Ollie knows anything about Joe."

"Yep, I'm on my way. See you."

Kerry put the phone down and resolved not to spend the rest of the evening getting worked up about Sonja and Natasha's new friendship. After all, there was no real reason to be so bothered...

Was there?

• • •

Joe woke up with a mouth like the Gobi Desert and a raging thirst. The inside of his head was exploding at two-second intervals. He was lying face down on top of his duvet and he had absolutely no idea how he'd got there.

He turned over and squinted at the Mickey Mouse clock on his wall. It said 7.30. Whether this was am or pm, Joe didn't know. It was daylight outside, but at this time of year that didn't mean a thing.

Hauling himself into a sitting position, Joe noticed that he was still fully clothed – he even had his dealer boots on. His upper body was wet through, for some reason, and he stank. Of what he wasn't sure, but it was a deeply unpleasant smell. It reminded him of walking through a dark alleyway that's been well used as a toilet.

Joe couldn't think why he smelt like that. He had little recollection of anything much at all, though it was obvious he'd been on another bender. His encounter with Catrina on Sunday hadn't helped his state of mind, but deep down Joe knew this was just an excuse. He'd been unhappy for ages. Years probably.

The worst thing was, he didn't know *why* he was so down on life. OK, so he was useless with girls, he had a complex about his looks, he was an oddball who didn't fit in, he often felt lonely, but was that *really* enough?

Joe often wondered if he was one of those people destined never to be happy, but he couldn't bear the thought of going through life in a sort of permanent depressed haze. He'd realised a while ago that if he drank himself stupid, he could forget for just a few hours.

The clash with Catrina had sent him from feeling reasonably confident about himself to the depths of despair. *That* was why he had gone out boozing on his own last night. And then...?

Well, he'd woken up in his bed with wet clothes on, feeling as if he'd been hit by a convoy of army trucks.

The thing that was worrying him most was *how* he'd got back home. Had he got here under his own steam or not? More importantly, had his mum seen him in such an obvious state and, if so, how livid was she going to be on a scale of one to ten when he emerged from his room?

Joe's mum was very protective of her son and extremely *involved*. Ever since his father had left home to live with another woman four years ago, Susie Gladwin had focused all her love and attention on her only child to suffocation point. Joe felt as if he was under scrutiny at all hours of the day and night.

His mum liked to take him shopping or go to the cinema with him. She'd probably even come to college with him if he let her. And when he did go out on his own, she wanted to know where he was going, who he was going with and what he was up to.

If she so much as smelt alcohol on his breath, she wanted to know how much he'd had, whether he was drunk (and if so, *why*) and whether he'd been 'getting up to any nonsense' with girls (if only!). Much as he loved his mum, he did wish she'd give him a bit more space.

Joe got out of bed very slowly and deliberately so as not to upset the balance of his fragile body. Last night wasn't the first time he'd been out of his head, but he'd never before felt so completely clueless about what had happened. Suddenly he felt out of control and it scared him.

As he got changed he concentrated hard, again trying to remember what had happened last night.

The only face he could recollect was Matt's. Where did he fit in?

Suddenly, Joe's stomach heaved with an awful sensation of queasiness. Dashing to the bathroom, he practically threw himself through the door. With his head stuck down the toilet, Joe had a vivid sense of *déjà vu*. He suddenly recalled being in Matt's garden... feeling very wet... throwing up.

With a great effort he focused his brain a little more and gradually began filling in the gaps...

CHAPTER 7

●●●●●●●●●●●●●●●●●●●●●●●●●●●●

TWO'S COMPANY...

"And she thought I'd make a brilliant model, said I had the right figure and face and *everything*!" Sonja stood in front of the full-length mirror in her room and studied her figure with appreciation.

"Natasha was convinced I'd be snapped up straight away if I went for it," she continued. "Isn't that great?"

Kerry lowered the magnified mirror she had been using to peer critically at her face. "It's *sickeningly* great," she replied, a touch of bitterness in her voice. "What did God think he was doing when he dished out people's looks?"

Sonja spun round to face her friend, a mystified look on her face. She wasn't entirely sure what Kerry was going on about.

"I mean, look at you," Kerry went on. "There

you are, tall, tanned and gorgeous. Perfect figure, looks to die for, nice teeth, shiny hair. You eat like a pig and stay stick thin. Then there's me..."

Kerry leapt up from the bed and stood in front of the mirror next to Sonja.

"Just look at it," she grumbled, stretching her arms out wide in despair. "Short, lumpy, fat thighs, huge arse, no boobs, hair I can't do a bloody thing with, blind as a bat. Complete stinking failure, actually!"

Sonja stared wide-eyed at her friend, astonished by the intensity of her unexpected outburst. Kerry was obviously having a Bad Hair Day, or suffering from PMT, or something.

"Don't be silly, Kez," she clucked, soothingly. "I don't know what you're complaining about – you're really attractive."

"Yeah, compared to a pig, perhaps!" Kerry took off her glasses and squinted into the mirror. A blurry blob with frizzy hair squinted back. "Mind you, not even pigs have got eyesight as bad as mine," she sighed dramatically.

"For God's sake, stop whingeing," Sonja chided. "I mean, it could be worse – you could look like Cat." She chuckled a little. "Now, as I was saying, Tasha was really encouraging. She said I had great bone structure, perfect for being a model. What do you think?"

"I think Natasha is absolutely right, you'd make a great model," Kerry said magnanimously. "If that's what you really want to do, then you should go for it."

"Well, that's the thing, isn't it? I don't, at least not in the long term."

"So *why* are you going on about it?" Kerry demanded a little irritably.

"I'm not! I just wanted your opinion, that's all. But if you're in such a foul mood I won't bother..."

Sonja gave Kerry a withering look which immediately made her friend wish she'd kept her mouth shut. Of course Sonja was right – she *was* in a foul mood and had been since she'd got to Sonja's house two hours ago.

They often met up at each other's homes to get ready for a night out together (mostly at Sonja's because she had more space). They usually had a couple of drinks while they got changed, experimented with different clothes, listened to CDs and generally got into the party mood.

But tonight, ever since Kerry had arrived, all Sonja had done was go on and on about blasted Natasha and what a 'laugh' they'd had the previous evening. She hadn't even thought to ask how Kerry was, what sort of day she'd had or anything remotely to do with anyone else.

And when Kerry had tried to change the subject and ask if there was any news about Joe, Sonja admitted that she and Natasha had been having *such* a great time at the café, she'd completely forgotten to call on Ollie. They'd even gone to the pictures together and caught the later showing of the film she was supposed to have seen with Matt.

"Ooh, come on, hurry up," Sonja announced looking at her watch. "I told Tasha we'd meet her at eight. Mustn't be late."

No, we couldn't possibly be late for Tasha, Kerry thought bitterly. *It wouldn't do to keep poor Tasha waiting, would it? Never mind that I've spent hours of my life waiting for Sonja to turn up because she's hardly ever on time. Oh no, suddenly we must all break our backs just because it's ruddy Natasha!*

Kerry deliberately took her time finishing her nails; she had already decided that this was going to be a really bad night out.

Sonja grabbed her bag from the dresser, opened the door and waved at Kerry to follow her, which she dutifully did. The girls then made the short walk to the bar where they had arranged to meet Natasha.

As she walked through the door, Kerry half

expected to see Matt or Catrina or one of the others. But tonight there were only the faces of people she barely knew. Oh, and Natasha sitting on a bar stool already being chatted up by a suave-looking older guy in a posh suit and tie.

Catching the girls' eyes as they walked in, Natasha pulled a 'help me' face over the guy's shoulder. Immediately taking the initiative, Sonja strode over to where they were sitting and touched Natasha's bare thigh.

"Sorry I'm late, darling," she cooed, "I got held up. I hope no one's been hassling you." She leant over and kissed Natasha on the lips.

The guy at the bar's eyes nearly popped out of his head while Kerry hung back in the doorway, deeply embarrassed by Sonja's spot of acting.

"Uh, no," Natasha replied, immediately cottoning on. "This is John. John – meet my girlfriend."

Crimson-faced, the poor guy was already beginning to beat a hasty retreat. Once he was out of sight, the duo collapsed in hysterics and the tone of the evening was set.

As Kerry had expected, it was the start of a rotten night playing second fiddle to the Sonja and Natasha show. And even though she couldn't find any particular reason to hate Ollie's sister, the fact that she and Sonja seemed to have such a good time together was enough to make Kerry retreat into a shell of unease in their company. The fact that they didn't even seem to notice that Kerry was there didn't improve the situation.

Half-way through the evening Natasha suggested they go to a club called Henry's.

"I used to go there all the time when I lived at home," she beamed. "I know Henry and he used to let me in even though I was only fourteen. He thought I was much older, tarted up in make-up and heels and little dresses. It was such a hoot! The music's great and there's always tasty guys there. C'mon, what do you say?"

Kerry didn't know what to say. Henry's had always looked a bit sleazy to her from the outside and she'd never had any desire to go in there at all.

"Oh wow, yeah, great! Let's go!" Sonja hollered before Kerry could think of a way to wriggle out of it.

Without bothering to find out what Kerry wanted to do, Natasha and Sonja left the bar and began heading up the street towards Henry's. Reluctantly, Kerry tagged along behind.

As soon as they got inside the club, Kerry's heart sank even further. The place had changed hands several times since Natasha had last been there and with dingy lighting, faded soft furnishings and floors that your feet stuck to as you walked, it looked as if it had seen better times.

Still, there was a dance floor and music – and that was all the girls needed really.

Sonja and Natasha immediately made a beeline for the dance floor and began grooving wildly to an obscure '70s track. In no mood to join them, Kerry found a seat on the edge of the dance floor, wishing she was at home with a cup of hot chocolate and a *Friends* video.

She had no idea that she was being watched.

CHAPTER 8

• •

... AND THREE'S A CROWD

Joe stood in a dimly-lit corner of the bar at Henry's and took in Kerry's every move. It didn't take much working out to realise that she was incredibly uncomfortable sitting there.

And no wonder, he thought. *What the heck is she doing in a dump like this?*

Joe had been coming to Henry's off and on for several weeks. It was an open-house kind of establishment where you could drink for twenty-four hours a day if that was what you wanted. He had been flabbergasted when he'd seen the girls walk in.

The only reason Joe came here was because it was so seedy it was unlikely that anyone he knew would ever set foot in the place. And that meant that his secret was less likely to be discovered.

But now? Now he would have to leave before he was spotted.

But Joe didn't want to go. The sight of Kerry looking so pretty, so lonely and so out of place made him long to walk up to her, talk to her – dance with her even.

But he knew he would never have the nerve to do any of those things. She would laugh in his face – any girl would.

No one in their right mind would want to dance with someone who (as Catrina had so rightly pointed out) was boring, dull, had no life and appalling dress sense.

Joe knocked back his drink, slid down from his stool and stumbled from the club.

● ● ●

This is awful, thought Kerry as she peered into the blackness around her, trying to make out what sort of place Henry's was. Her eyes scanned the dingily-lit room.

Apart from the dance floor and the six or seven people on it, there didn't appear to be much other life in the place.

There were a couple of scruffy-looking guys sitting at a table in one corner, and a few blokes at the bar, but apart from that, no one.

What on earth was she doing in such a dump? Kerry's mood became blacker by the second.

The thing that angered her *more* than the fact that she was in a dirty little dive that stank of stale beer and toilets, was that Sonja and Natasha were obviously having such a great time. They had barely said a word to Kerry all evening – they'd just danced and laughed and whispered together like a couple of silly schoolgirls. God, they were infuriating!

Kerry looked at her watch. Only 11.30 pm. Maybe she should say she felt sick, then she could call a cab and leave the party animals to it. The idea appealed enormously.

Just as she was about try and get Sonja's attention, Natasha came bounding off the dance floor.

"God, this place is crap!" Natasha laughed as she plonked herself down opposite Kerry.

"What do you mean?" Kerry frowned. "I thought you were having a good time?"

"Oh, I am. I'm having a brilliant time," Natasha explained. "I haven't had such a good laugh in ages. But this place is just *so* grim. Have you noticed the kind of weirdos that are in here?"

"No other type, is there? Anyway, where's Sonja gone?"

"To find the loo." Natasha looked around the

dingy room. "Y'know, this place used to be dripping with fit guys. I can't believe it's gone downhill like this. I'm really sorry to have dragged you both here."

"Don't worry – it's been an experience, I guess. And at least we'll know not to come here again."

Kerry smiled at Natasha and felt a little guilty about the negative thoughts she'd been harbouring.

Natasha actually seemed to be a very nice person. If she had a bone to pick with anyone, it should be Sonja since it was she who was being so completely insensitive to Kerry's feelings.

Or was Sonja just being typically Sonja – boisterous and flighty and out for a good time with anyone who cared to come along? Maybe Kerry was just being oversensitive...

Kerry was coming to the conclusion that perhaps she wouldn't pretend to be ill after all. Perhaps she ought to just throw herself into the evening and have a good time. Sort of, if you can't beat 'em, join 'em.

Just then Sonja came back.

"You won't believe what just happened," she gabbled excitedly. "That guy over there just asked me if I wanted something to make me feel good..."

"*What*? What did he mean?" Kerry was confused.

"Drugs?" asked Natasha, cottoning on immediately.

"I guess so," Sonja replied, looking at Natasha, goggle-eyed. "I told him I felt good enough without them, thank you very much, which I don't think he appreciated."

Natasha giggled into the back of her hand while Kerry frowned. Now she knew this place was the pits. To have total strangers come up to you and offer you drugs was awful. This club obviously attracted just the sort of people Kerry didn't want to be mixing with. She got up from her seat.

"Right, that's it, I'm going," she announced determinedly. "I'm not staying in this dump a second longer."

Natasha stood up too. "Yeah, I think you're right," she said. "Anyway, there's not one fit guy here so I guess we're wasting our time. Do you fancy going on somewhere else?"

"No way!" Kerry groaned, at the same time as Sonja squealed "Yeaaah!"

Hearing Kerry's objection, Sonja added, "Oh come *on*, Kez, don't be such a bore! We could go to that new club that's opened down by the bus station. You know – Enigma. It's supposed to be *the* place to go now."

Kerry was incensed.

How *dare* Sonja call her a bore! If anyone was boring it was *her*.

At least Kerry didn't spend her entire life thinking only about herself. Now *that* was boring and as far as she was concerned, it was one of Sonja's worst traits. Along with the insensitivity, brashness and the fact that she was a completely disloyal, flighty, fickle, fly-by-night *friend*.

Kerry stopped short of voicing her opinions. Instead, she counted to ten and gave a strained little smile in Sonja's direction.

"I really think I'm going to go home," she said calmly, "however boring that may be. Why don't I walk with you to the taxi rank, then I'll get a cab and you two can go on and have a good time? I really don't feel up to going anywhere else now. I'm whacked. And I'm sure you'll have a much better time without me."

There. Kerry the diplomat came through just in time. If Sonja knew what she was really feeling right now, they might not have a friendship left. And Kerry was torn between anger and insecurity – she may be livid inside, but she didn't want to lose Sonja as a best friend.

"*Well*, if you're sure," Sonja said, a little too quickly for Kerry's liking.

"I'm sure. I'll call round and collect my things some time tomorrow, if that's OK."

Kerry picked up her bag and began walking towards the exit. No one noticed the tears in her eyes as she strode purposefully ahead.

CHAPTER 9

● ●

MISSING, PRESUMED LATE

Kerry woke up feeling as if her head was stuffed with cotton wool and her eyes had been glued shut. She squeezed them hard for a few seconds then headed for the bathroom for some Nurofen and a shower.

Studying her face in the bathroom mirror, Kerry was horrified by the puffy-eyed, mascara-stained monster who stared back at her. After snivelling all the way home in the taxi last night, she had gone straight to bed for a good old howl of self-pity. And left her make-up on.

Now, in a rather more rational frame of mind, she realised that she had probably over-reacted to the events of the past couple of days. So what if Sonja thought Natasha was the most fascinating, fun-loving person on earth? It was completely ridiculous that Kerry should feel threatened by her.

It wasn't as though she was around all the time and intent on stealing Sonja away. She'd be going back to London soon and might not be seen in Winstead again for months. That wasn't the sort of relationship that was going to threaten the friendship Sonja and Kerry had built up over the last twelve years.

And there was no avoiding the fact that Sonja was much more of a party animal than Kerry. She was bound to get on with someone who could match her step for step on the dance floor.

Kerry stepped into the shower and vowed not to let any of this stuff get to her any more. She was due to meet some of the gang at the café in an hour, and if Natasha was there too, then great. Kerry was determined to be level-headed about this; she was not going to let jealousy get in the way.

In fact, when Kerry got to the End, Natasha wasn't there. Nor was anyone else.

Odd! thought Kerry. She was sure they'd arranged to meet at midday. It was only ten past twelve – surely someone should have turned up by now.

She went up to the counter to see who was on duty today.

"Hello? Anna! Are you there?"

"On my way," she heard Ollie's voice call from somewhere behind her.

Turning around, she saw his body reversing into the café from the street outside, his arms cradling what seemed like several hundred loaves of bread.

"Oh, hi Kez. Good, I'm glad you're here. I haven't got enough arms. Could you do us a favour and lift up that worktop there so I can get these into the kitchen?"

Kerry reached under the counter and felt for the bolt. She slid it across and lifted up the stainless steel worktop to let Ollie through. Holding it aloft, she watched as he struggled sideways through the gap, his head tilted back and his chin delicately positioned to steady the pyramid of bread.

Just as he was about to clear the gap, Kerry lost her grip on the worktop and watched in horror as it fell, clonking Ollie with a hefty thwack on the back of his head.

"Eurrrgh!" Ollie cried. His head jerked forward and the tower of loaves tumbled in all directions.

The next thing Kerry knew, he was on his knees, grovelling among a sea of white bread, fiercely rubbing the back of his head and groaning softly to himself.

"Oh, Ollie, I'm so sorry!" Kerry yelped, holding her hand to her mouth in absolute horror.

God, what a clumsy cow, she thought. *I can't believe I just did that! What a stupid, dumb-arsed thing to do. And of all people, it had to be Ollie. Poor Ollie!*

Kerry knelt down beside Ollie, who was crouched in pain, unsure of what to do.

"Are you OK?" she mumbled. "Can I do anything?"

Ollie didn't answer. He just sat rubbing his head, his face crimson.

"I'm *so* sorry!" Kerry wailed. "It just slipped out of my hand. It was an accident."

Still no response. Kerry wondered if he was seriously hurt.

"Can you hear me, Ollie?" she asked tentatively, poking him in the arm.

Ollie's face contorted into an involuntary grimace that he struggled to turn into a smile. "You sound like someone out of ER," he croaked at last.

"Sorry," Kerry babbled. "I'm *really* sorry..."

Ollie gave Kerry a wry grin. "If you stop saying sorry for a second perhaps you could get me a towel or something to put on the lump that's erupting from the back of my head."

Kerry leapt up and ran towards the kitchen.

Going through the door she tripped on a loaf of bread and went flying herself, landing on the floor with a thud.

Oh no, this is just awful, she thought as she lay looking at the terracotta floor tiles and reddening with embarrassment. *Why did this have to happen now, with Ollie? Why couldn't it have been Anna who I just tried to kill? Or Nick? Anyone other than Ollie...*

Then she heard a loud guffaw and, looking around, saw Ollie creased up with hysterical laughter. She had to admit that they did look a rare old spectacle, like extras in a bad disaster movie. Kerry's look of torture brightened into a massive grin and she crawled her way back to Ollie. They sat leaning against one other, unable to speak because they were laughing so much.

"Oh, Ollie, I'm really sorry..." said Kerry for the umpteenth time once she'd got her breath back. "I only came in to meet the others."

"You've just missed them," Ollie explained. "They've gone down to the river for a picnic. Took all of yesterday's left-over sandwiches, a load of crisps and fizzy drinks. Maya tried to call you at home but you must have already left." Kerry's face went from girlish joy to a look of hurt and disappointment.

"Oh. So they went on without me. Was Sonja here too?"

Ollie nodded. "She came in with Tasha. She stayed at Sonja's last night."

"Oh."

"Didn't you know? I thought you went out with them too?"

"I did, but I went home early," Kerry told him. "Oh, Ollie, it was awful. I might as well not have been there. Your sister and Sonja were acting like a couple of long-lost pals all night."

"And that got to you, did it?"

"It did at the time. Then I decided I'd been over-reacting. But now I'm not so sure."

"Don't let it bug you," Ollie consoled. "Sonja and Natasha are way too similar to get along in the long term. Why do you think they gave each other such a wide berth at school? Neither of them has changed that much. They'll get sick of the sight of each other soon. Trust me."

Ollie gave Kerry's hand a little squeeze which made her blush. If he noticed he chose to ignore it, adding, "Now, are you going to go and meet the others? I'll make you a cheese and tomato sandwich – on the house. And I've got a custard slice left over. You've only missed them by five minutes and I said I'd fill you in on the details. They're down by the watermill."

"Oh, I don't know," Kerry mumbled. "I'm not sure I can be bothered now."

"Look, you must. You'll have a great time."

"Uh, OK. Who else is there?"

"Matt, Maya, Sonja, Tasha and Cat."

"What about Joe?"

"Dunno." Ollie frowned. "You haven't seen him, have you?"

"No. You know about Matt finding him drunk the other day though, don't you?"

"Yeah. I keep trying to find him to ask what happened, but he's never in. He's been acting a bit weird lately, but he won't talk about it."

"What do you mean, weird?"

"I dunno really, I can't explain..." Ollie paused, trying to find the right words as he got to his feet and expertly threw Kelly's sandwich together. "...He's just not himself. He's kind of sullen, withdrawn. I know he's like that a lot of the time with other people, but not with me. He knows he can talk to me. But I've hardly seen him these last couple of weeks. It's just odd."

"I'll keep a look out for him." promised Kerry, dusting herself off. "So, are you gonna come to the river when you knock off here?"

"Possibly. Elaine's coming over today but I'm not sure when. If she gets here by the time my shift ends, we'll come along."

"Great..." Kerry felt a stab of disappointment. Typical! Not only had she lost her best friend to someone else, but now her best male friend had his girlfriend tagging along too. It sounded like an afternoon made in hell. Still, she had nothing better to do.

Taking the food Ollie was holding out for her, Kerry turned and headed for the river.

CHAPTER 10

● ●

KERRY GRITS HER TEETH

When Kerry found the others they greeted her like a long-lost friend.

"Kez, thank God you got the message!" Maya cried, leaping up from the grassy bank and rushing forward to greet her.

"Yeah, about time too," added Matt. "We thought you weren't coming."

"Sonja reckoned you'd been abducted by aliens on your way home last night when you didn't turn up at the café," Cat cackled.

"But I *did* get to the café," Kerry countered. "At just after twelve."

"And you were supposed to be there at eleven thirty on the dot," Matt said. "We can't sit around all day waiting for you to sort your hair out, you know."

Sonja broke off from her conversation with Natasha and turned to Kerry.

"I waited as long as I could, Kez," she said. "I thought you knew we were meeting at eleven thirty."

Kerry seethed inwardly. She distinctly remembered Sonja telling her to get to the café at twelve.

Had Sonja deliberately told her the wrong time? Kerry couldn't be sure. She counted to ten (really quickly) and decided it wasn't worth starting a fight.

"I, uh, must have misheard you, Son," she relented, practically choking on her words. "So... have I missed anything?"

"No, apart from Matt trying to have sex with anyone who's willing," Catrina said through a haze of cigarette smoke.

"Yeah, I feel really rampant at the moment and I think this could be your lucky day, Kez." Striking an exaggerated Love God pose, Matt strutted up to Kerry and began running his outstretched arms up and down her body in mock passion.

"So what you're saying is that you've had no takers so far," grinned Kerry and then blushed, immediately embarrassed by her reply.

"In a word, yes," said Catrina on Matt's behalf.

"But it's not *fair*," Matt wailed, all fake angst

and bad acting. "I'm so ugly and still a virgin and *nobody* wants me!"

It was the sort of performance only someone as good-looking and super-confident as Matt could get away with. And being the only male in the company of girls this afternoon – and loving every minute of it – he was letting them know how much he rated himself.

"Have you ever considered developing a personality? I hear it can work wonders with the *laydeez*, you know." Catrina smirked.

"Hey, who needs a personality when you've got looks like mine?" Matt replied, thrusting out his pelvis and running his hand through his hair.

"You said it," Maya laughed.

Kerry sat down on the grass between Maya and Sonja who immediately turned her back on Kerry to carry on chatting to Natasha. But Kerry was determined to make an effort.

"So, did you guys have a good time last night?" she asked, smiling.

Sonja glanced over her shoulder at Kerry. "Mmmm, great, thanks."

"Did you go to that new club then?"

"Uh, no, we just ended up at another couple of bars..."

"Meet any guys?"

"Only dorks."

"So I didn't miss much then?"

"Nope."

"What time did you get home?"

"Uh... not sure, two-ish?"

"Oh, so you didn't end up on an all-nighter then?"

"No."

"Oh." Kerry was running out of questions to ask and it wasn't as if she was getting any help from Sonja.

She watched helplessly as Sonja leaned over to Natasha and whispered something in her ear. The pair then collapsed into fits of giggles. Kerry looked on, bemused and hurt, and felt tears pricking her eyes again. She couldn't work out whether they were sharing some secret about the night before or laughing at her.

When they'd finally stopped sniggering, Sonja and Natasha huddled together once more and began talking in hushed tones, punctuated by the occasional titter.

Talk about rude! Kerry thought, gritting her teeth and trying not to let it get to her. She spent much of the next couple of hours chatting to everyone except Sonja and Natasha, who continued their own, very private, conversation.

• • •

Kerry spotted Ollie and Elaine first, walking along the towpath, hand in hand, a picture of syrupy contentment. It was at times like this, when she saw someone she knew so happy and in love, that Kerry really wished *she* had a boyfriend. Especially someone as nice as Ollie. Elaine was lucky to have bagged a catch like him; she often wondered if Elaine realised that or whether she took him for granted.

Frankly, Kerry couldn't fathom quite what kept things going between the pair. They both insisted that the relationship was a very relaxed one, with no ties. But Kerry reckoned that it must be pretty solid to stand the separation.

Elaine lived about sixty miles away, and neither she nor Ollie had a car. When they did get together, they always looked so pleased to be in each other's company. Kerry was convinced – they had to be in love.

"Hi, Elaine," Maya called out. "We haven't seen you since Ollie's gig at The Bell. What have you been up to?"

"You don't need to ask her that," Matt cut in. "It should be obvious. She'll have been out in people's back gardens saving the woodlice, or bonding with tree people and playing with her crystals all at the same time. Isn't that right, E?"

Elaine beamed. She knew Matt was sending

her up and she didn't mind one bit. They got on really well despite being complete opposites. Matt was a capitalist, would-be entrepreneur, while Elaine was a bit of a hippy – but they sparked off each other whenever they met.

"Actually, I'm into nose cogency at the moment. It's the latest thing," she said. "You can get a lot of negative energy from your nose which you can channel into the positive if you stick your finger up high enough. It would probably work for *you*, Matt, if you stuck it up your backside."

The banter carried on like this for the rest of the afternoon. Only Sonja and Natasha didn't join in; they seemed to have so much to talk about between themselves. One or the other might give the occasional conspiratorial glance round at the rest of the gang, but other than that they were totally engrossed in what the other had to say.

After a while, Kerry could bear it no longer.

"I think I'll go for a walk," she announced to no one in particular, standing up.

"I'll come," said Ollie, surprising Kerry so much that she blushed.

"Uh... uh, how about you, Elaine?" Kerry asked quickly.

Elaine, who was deep in conversation with

Matt, lifted her head and looked vaguely in Kerry's direction.

"Sorry, what?"

"Do you want to come for a walk?"

"Um, I don't think I will, thanks. I'm a bit whacked, actually."

"Anyone else?" Kerry asked.

Without waiting for a response, Ollie set off down the towpath.

"Come on, Kez," he called. "It's just you and me."

● ● ●

"You seemed pretty peed off back there." Ollie gave Kerry a look of real concern as they walked side by side along the towpath.

"You could tell? I thought I was being subtle."

"You were. But I know what's been going through your head these last few days, don't I?"

Kerry sighed. "I guess so. To be perfectly honest, Ollie, I'm getting pretty sick of Sonja. She's completely ignoring me. Do you think I've upset her? Is she punishing me for something, 'cause if she is I wish she'd spit it out. She's driving me nuts."

"Come on, you know Sonja better than that. If she was hacked off with you, you'd know about it. She's not the sort to hide her feelings, is she?"

Ollie raised his eyebrows at Kerry and she shook her head.

"She's a bit like a puppy," he continued. You know – all in-your-face enthusiasm and charm, wanting to lark about with anyone who'll join in. She doesn't mean anything by it, I'm sure. She won't even have realised that you're fed up, Sonja doesn't consider anyone's feelings other than her own."

Ollie shot another considerate look at his friend, and added, "Your trouble is you're too sensitive – you need to lighten up a bit."

"You're right of course," Kerry shrugged. "And in my more rational moments I can see that and convince myself that their sudden friendship doesn't bother me. But the truth is, it does."

She stopped – aware that the conversation was getting a bit heavy for a Sunday afternoon picnic. She tried to lighten up a bit.

"I must have some jealousy problem that stems from childhood – maybe the fact that Lewis was born so long after me made me feel like he stole my parents' attention. Maybe since then I've had a problem with sharing things. Like my friends."

Kerry gave a Ollie a wry grin to let him know she was trying not to take herself too seriously, and he responded by putting his arm around her shoulders for a moment and giving her a comforting squeeze. Which made her blush again.

They carried on walking in silence for a while.

What a lovely day, thought Kerry as she studied the glints of white light the sun's reflection made on the surface of the river beside her. The only noise they could hear was the *plip! plop! plop!* of the stones Ollie was skimming across the water's surface, and the occasional "yeess!" that came from his lips when he'd thrown a particularly good one.

He's like a little kid sometimes, she thought. *Totally engrossed in his game and not taking a blind bit of notice where he's walking. He'll stand in some dog poo soon*, she giggled to herself.

Kerry's attention was suddenly caught by a figure making its way down the steps from the lane to the river. From behind Kerry thought it looked like a boy.

What made him stand out was the way he was walking. Having reached the towpath, he meandered about ahead of them as if he was drunk, stumbling a couple of times as he walked. When the boy turned to look across the river Kerry could see his face in profile.

It was Joe.

CHAPTER 11

●●●●●●●●●●●●●●●●●●●●●●●●●●

SURELY NOT JOE?

"Ollie? Ollie! Look!"

Kerry ran towards Ollie, who was poking around on the ground for more stones to skim, and tugged at the sleeve of his T-shirt. He looked to where she was pointing and, although he could only see the rear view, immediately recognised his best friend.

"Oh, yeah, it's Joe," he said, his face breaking into a grin.

Moments later, his expression changed to a deep frown as he took in the way Joe was lurching from side to side.

"Joe? Hey, Joe!"

Kerry could hear the concern in Ollie's voice as he began to sprint towards the sorry-looking figure ahead of him.

Joe stopped, turned round deliberately and looked behind him. Seeing Ollie chasing up the path, closely followed by Kerry, he made his way slowly to the grassy bank and sat down.

Ollie stopped short at the sight of his friend. Joe looked ill. His messy brown hair was lank and greasy, his skin was grey and his eyes had black circles under them.

"Hey, mate, are you OK?" Ollie asked tentatively, sitting on the bank next to Joe. Anyone could see that Joe was far from OK, but Ollie knew him well enough not to push him into a corner with confrontational questions.

"Sure," Joe replied. "I'm great. Feel good. Life's a blast..."

His voice trailed off as he looked past Ollie to some point in the distance. He stared vacantly ahead, lost in thought.

Kerry and Ollie glanced at each other, worry lines etched deep on both their faces.

"Hey, would either of you guys like a drink?" Joe dug deep into the pocket of his combats and pulled out a small Evian bottle half full of what looked like water.

Immediately suspicious, Ollie took a sip from the bottle and pulled a face. There *was* water in the bottle, but the overriding taste was of vodka.

"It's a little early for me, mate," said Ollie,

passing the bottle back to his friend. "I didn't realise you were a vodka drinker."

"Neither did I," Joe replied and giggled. He was obviously finding something amusing, though both Ollie and Kerry were at a loss to see what was so funny.

"I haven't seen you around for a while," Ollie continued, his friendly tone concealing his anxiety. "What have you been up to?"

"Uh, this and that. Nothing special. Out clubbing, having a few drinks, meeting up with some people..." Joe stopped, as if to collect his thoughts before continuing.

"Me and Jim went to this place last night... you could buy triple hamburgers for a pound, I think. I had seventeen. It was cold yesterday, wasn't it? For the time of year. I, uh..."

He stopped again, and began fiddling with the lace of one of his boots, studying it intently.

Ollie started to feel scared, *really* scared. Who was Jim? What was Joe talking about? He had never seen his friend in such a state. He was totally out of it, talking complete, rambling gibberish. Ollie knew Joe had been feeling down recently, but he had no idea of the depth of his friend's depression.

He must have it pretty bad to be using drink as an escape, Ollie thought.

Ollie knew he had to do something, but he didn't know what. He was also experiencing overwhelming feelings of guilt for allowing his friend get into such a state. For not even noticing that something was obviously so badly wrong in Joe's life that he could end up like *this*. Ollie had to act before it was too late.

Joe was lying flat out on the river bank now, his eyes closed, humming away to himself, his feet tapping in time to some tune in his head. It wasn't too long before he was asleep, snoring softly.

"I can't believe he's so drunk," Kerry whispered to Ollie. "He could've fallen in the river and drowned if we hadn't come along. Shall I go and ask Matt to bring his car along so we can get him home?"

Ollie shook his head. He didn't want anyone else to know about this.

"No, no way. Look, Kez, you go back to the others while I try and get Joe home."

"Oh, OK. But what should I tell them?"

"Anything so long as it's not the truth." He immediately saw that Kerry looked uncomfortable with the idea of telling lies.

"We mustn't let anyone know about this, Kerry." There was an urgency in Ollie's voice that Kerry hadn't heard before. "Joe needs our help and the less people know, the easier it will be to get him back on track. I reckon the last thing he needs right now is to be the focus of attention. Joe would hate that."

Kerry nodded – she knew he was right.

"Tell them I've gone off to get more food and drink. I'll get back as quick as I can."

Ollie began shaking Joe to wake him up. "Hey, Joe, come on, wakey wakey!"

"Oh, man, I'm whacked," Joe mumbled to no one in particular, eyes still firmly shut.

"Yeah, I know the feeling," Ollie said. "I've done too many shifts at the café and record shop over the last few days. I think I'll head for home. How about you, Kez?"

"Um, I think I'll go back to the others," she said, standing up and brushing grass off her jeans.

"What about you, Joe?" Ollie carried on. "Actually, I wanted to talk to you about a couple of gigs we've got coming up. And I've penned in a date for rehearsals next Friday. Why don't you come back with me so we can talk about it?"

Joe opened his eyes and squinted into the sunlight. "Yeah, sure, Ol. Whatever you say." He struggled to get to his feet.

Not wanting to make a big thing of the state Joe was in, Ollie pretended not to notice.

When they got back to the steps where Kerry had first spotted Joe, she carried on walking while Ollie split off in the direction of his home. A mumbling, stumbling Joe followed him, blissfully unaware of the concern his friends felt for him.

CHAPTER 12

. . . .

CAT GETS STUCK IN

Catrina was bored with the picnic. Matt was sitting by the river talking to Sonja and Natasha about his favourite subject – himself. Maya and Elaine were having a serious discussion about eco warriors, and heaven only knew where Ollie and Kerry had got to. Cat was beginning to doze off in the sun.

"Right, you guys," she announced briskly as she stood up. "I'm off. I've got a hot date with a fireman tonight, so I must go and tart myself up."

Cat was lying, of course – she often did – but there was no way she was admitting that she had a pile of ironing to do for her mother before tomorrow. The lie just tripped off her tongue without her having to think about it too much.

The others said their goodbyes as she left to

make her way back to the flat she shared with her mum on the east side of town. As she walked down the main road back into Winstead, she spotted Ollie and Joe on the pavement opposite.

Great! she thought. *Someone to chat to on the way back.*

"Hey, Ollie! Joe!" Teetering along in her clumpy shoes, Catrina wobbled across the road.

Ollie's heart began to pound at the sound of that distinctive voice. An audience with Catrina Osgood was the last thing he and Joe needed right now. If she sussed something was up with Joe – and it wouldn't take a rocket scientist to work things out – it would be all round town before Joe had a chance to take his next breath.

But there was no escape. Seconds later, Cat was upon them.

"Hey, didn't you hear me calling?" she said, grabbing Ollie by the arm and linking it with hers so that they were walking three abreast.

"Uh, sorry, Cat, we were talking," Ollie lied, praying that with him in the middle, Catrina wouldn't notice Joe's dishevelled appearance.

No such luck. Cat leaned forward to speak to Joe then stopped dead in her tracks.

"My God, Joe!" she shrieked. "What the hell's the matter with you?"

Cat hadn't seen Joe since that day in the park

when she'd tried to pinch his notepad; he was hardly recognisable now.

Since leaving the river with Ollie, Joe had gone from talking complete rubbish to not talking at all. He'd stared blankly ahead, allowing Ollie to guide him down the road like a frail old man.

Now Catrina's screeching shook him out of his catatonic state.

"Wh-what?!" Joe focused on the girl and was surprised to see the look of horror on her face.

Catrina stood in front of Joe, blocking his path, and looked him up and down, weighing up the situation. Joe swayed gently in front of her. Then she noticed Ollie's air of unease, as though he was wishing for all the world that she wasn't there.

"You're out of it, aren't you, Joe?" she snapped. "Whatever happened to Mr Boring, Mr Whiter-than-white Joey Gladwin? You lied to me at the barbie, Joe. You said you didn't drink. Now you look like you belong with the tramps and meths heads down by the Sidings."

She was referring to the small band of homeless people, mostly alcoholics and drug users, who lived rough at the seedy end of town. The reference made Ollie seethe.

"Shut up, Cat. You don't know what you're talking about," he snapped.

"Don't you believe it, Ollie. You have no idea. I know damn well what I'm talking about, actually, I've seen it all before." Catrina was red in the face now and Ollie could see the anger in her eyes. He didn't think he'd ever seen her this livid – she was practically breathing fire.

"What exactly do you mean, Cat?" he demanded.

"That's none of your business. But I bet I know a whole lot more than the pair of you put together. And take it from me, Joe, by my reckoning you've got very little time left to sort yourself out."

Cat reached out and prodded Joe in the chest. "Look at you! You're pathetic, standing there out of your head. Was it worth it, Joe? *Is* it worth the mess you must be making of your life?"

Joe concentrated his gaze on Catrina, now with her hands on her hips, mouthing off like a high court judge. He suddenly felt totally lucid and, for the first time ever, he wasn't frightened of her.

Joe took a step nearer to Cat. He was shaking with anger as he spoke.

"While you're standing there playing God, perhaps you would just remember this. You and your big gob have helped make me like this, you fat tart."

He came a little closer so that his face almost

touched Cat's. "Think about that the next time you decide to bad-mouth someone to their face. And in the meantime, WILL YOU GET OFF MY CASE?!!"

Then Joe turned on his heel and lurched off up a side street.

Moments later, Catrina burst into tears and ran in the opposite direction.

● ● ●

As Joe gradually sobered up at home, he began to feel bad about the way he had shouted at Catrina. Studying the reflection of the stranger staring back at him from his bedroom mirror, he realised that she might have a point.

He had avoided looking at himself recently; he knew he looked rough and didn't need reminding of it. Now, the sight was enough to shock him into some hard thinking.

Although the drinking had begun as a bit of an escape to start with – just the odd binge to help him forget his wretched life for a few hours – before he realised, he was drinking heavily every night, then at lunchtime, then both.

He was intelligent enough to know it wasn't doing him any good and he hated himself more with each greedy gulp he took. Yet it did help to dull the overwhelming feelings of self-doubt and depression that he suffered at most times, so it was difficult to find a sound enough reason to stop.

The memory of him shaking with anger as he'd turned on Catrina brought home the depth of his emotions. He peered even closer at his face in the mirror.

"What is your problem, Joe?" he asked. And sighed.

If I knew that, I'd have all the answers, he thought. *I'm an emotional screw-up, a complete waste of space. No one understands me – even Ollie doesn't know half the stuff that goes on in my head. And what chance does Kerry have of getting to know and like me when I don't know or like myself?*

"You know what you need?" he told the guy in the mirror. "You need to get a life!"

Except that I've got a life... of sorts, he thought. *It's just that it's fairly crap. I've got a mum who smothers me so much I might as well be back in the womb, a dad who's not around and not interested, so-called friends I can't even hold a conversation with. If it wasn't for Ollie and Kerry, I might have topped myself by now. No wonder I get out of my head... who else would want a life like mine?*

"Not me, mate," he sneered into the mirror, tears welling up in his eyes. He pointed an accusatory finger at himself. "You need to get back to reality and sort yourself out, Joe Gladwin. Before it's too late."

CHAPTER 13

● ●

OLLIE GETS A PROPOSAL

Ollie would have chased after Joe if it hadn't been for the fact that Catrina had only managed to wobble a little way down the road before she'd tripped over in her heels and gone flying. Much as he would have liked to leave the mouthy cow sprawled on her face, the sight of her blubbing like a baby brought out Ollie's soft-hearted streak and he went over and gently heaved her up.

Catrina grabbed Ollie's arm for support, rubbed a bloody knee and continued snivelling.

"So what was all that about back there?" Ollie asked, clearly bewildered by her vicious outburst. Cat didn't answer.

"Come on," Ollie continued, a little more agitated. "Joe's obviously having a hard enough time as it is without you coming along and sticking your nose in. There must have been a reason for it."

Catrina unhooked herself from Ollie's arm, gave herself a quick brush down and headed off down the road.

"Don't push it, Ollie," she snapped over her shoulder. "You don't know a thing about me and you never will."

Ollie sighed deeply and began rubbing his temples as he watched her flounce off in a huff. He realised he had a cracking headache and enough stress to last a lifetime, let alone an afternoon. He wondered what Cat meant... then started worrying about where Joe was – a much more pressing issue.

Then, realising Joe could be anywhere, and that it was unlikely that he'd find him, Ollie slowly made his way back to the remains of the picnic. Knowing his luck so far, he wouldn't have been surprised if they'd all gone home.

In fact, when Ollie did get back they were still there.

"So where are all these goodies you were supposed to be bringing?" Matt called.

Ollie had completely forgotten his story about going to fetch food and drink. He had to make his pounding head think fast.

"I... er, that's why I was so long, you see. I've

been to three places looking for stuff, but they were all closed 'cause it's after four o'clock. I got back as quick as I could."

"Another five minutes and you would have missed us, mate," said Matt. "We're all just about to go. Cat's already abandoned us and gone home."

Yeah and don't I know it... Ollie thought ruefully as he went up to Elaine and planted a kiss on her lips.

"Sorry, E," he said. "I really didn't mean to be gone for such an age."

"No worries, Ol," she smiled. "Maybe we could stop for a pizza or something on our way home."

"Sure, whatever you want."

Ollie glanced over at Kerry, who was sitting with Maya, her back to Sonja and Natasha. She gave him a look that asked *is everything all right?* to which he smiled and nodded, even though it wasn't.

• • •

Ollie must have apologised another three times for his prolonged absence as he and Elaine walked towards Pizza Hut together.

"I feel awful," he said. "We've spent hardly

any time together this afternoon. You came all this way just to end up talking to my mates."

"It really doesn't matter," Elaine repeated, also for at least the third time. "It's not like we're joined at the hip. Anyway, I've got a proposition to make that would mean us spending a lot more time together."

"Oh yeah, what?" Ollie was intrigued.

"We–ell..." Elaine looked him straight in the eye. "I've decided that I'm going to take some time out to go travelling for a year, maybe longer. Why don't you come too?"

Ollie was taken aback – this was absolutely *not* what he'd expected to hear. He knew Elaine had been hankering to see more of the world for some time, but he had no idea it was so serious or that it would happen this soon. *Or* that she would want to involve him.

"Oh, Ollie, it would be brilliant," she continued. "We'd have such a fabulous time. Just imagine actually being in all those countries you've only ever seen on the telly – Australia, America, Russia! It would just be the most fantastic experience, a once-in-a-lifetime opportunity."

Ollie wasn't sure how to react and he didn't want to commit himself until he'd given the idea a lot more thought. Anyway, he suddenly realised, what the heck was he doing even *considering* such an outlandish offer when he didn't have a bean to pay for it?

He put his arm around Elaine's shoulder and drew her towards him.

"It sounds great, E," he said softly, "but it also sounds expensive. And I'm skint. I couldn't even afford a bus ticket to Brighton at the moment, let alone fly to the other side of the world."

"Ah, well, that's where I come in," she beamed. "Because you know my great aunt who died a couple of months back?"

Ollie nodded.

"Well, she only left me a load of money in her will. Enough for a couple of round-the-world tickets, plus a bit left over. So you don't have to worry about that at all!"

Elaine paused a second to see the effect of her words, before continuing. "And once we're out there we could both get jobs in whatever country we're in. There's always bar work or fruit-picking or something – we could do *anything* if we set our minds to it. And anyway, what have you got to keep you here?"

"Well, there's my jobs at the café and the record shop..."

"What, a couple of grotty jobs in the dullest of towns and absolutely nothing to look forward to?

Come on, Ollie! You could work in a café anywhere in the world and get to see all those great places as well. So what do you say?"

Elaine's cheeks were flushed and her eyes sparkling. Ollie could see that she was really fired up over this one, and he had to admit that she was painting a very attractive picture for him.

It was just such a shock announcement out of the blue, and an offer he wouldn't have dreamed would come his way in an entire lifetime.

"I, uh, I'm a bit gobsmacked to be honest, E," Ollie finally responded. "It sounds brilliant, it really does. But it's such a big thing, I really ought to give it some serious thought. I can't say yes just like that. I mean, there's a lot to consider. Anyway, what about you and university? What about your parents? What have they got to say about it?"

"Mum's dead jealous. She says it was what she'd have liked to do if she hadn't got pregnant with me so young. And uni can wait. They've already said they'll defer my place for a year so that's not a problem at all."

"So, uh, when are you thinking of going?"

"As soon as I can get the tickets and visas and injections and all that stuff sorted. I suppose realistically it'll be in a month or so."

"And if I decide not to come?"

"Then I'll go anyway. Seriously. Look, Ollie, I'm eighteen, I've got my whole life ahead of me, but at this present moment I have no ties."

Elaine's voice became very earnest as she squeezed Ollie's arm. "This is absolutely the best time to do it, you know – there's nothing to keep me here. Only you. And that's why I want you to come with me."

"Aw, that's really sweet," Ollie answered, hugging her even closer. "I am tempted. And it really is lovely of you to offer to pay for the ticket. Maybe my parents would help stump up some more cash..." He trailed off and they continued to walk in silence, wrapped up in their thoughts of faraway places.

"Y'know," Ollie carried on after a while, "it'd be so cool to be able to look back on your life and say you'd been to all those countries that most people only get to dream about. You'd have so many new experiences to tell people about. In some ways it'd be really weird coming back to Winstead after so much had happened to you while you were away, and yet nothing had changed when you got back. It'd be like re-entering a time warp."

"Who's to say we would come back, Ollie?" Elaine smiled, then looked seriously at him. "Who knows what might happen? We might find we love a place so much that we want to stay there... you know, get jobs, invent new lives for ourselves. We might not ever want to come back home."

CHAPTER 14

● ●

WILL HE, WON'T HE?

Ollie was troubled. He had been ever since Elaine had left on Monday morning. Now, sitting in his room above The Swan, he was even more anxious.

Initially, he had been intrigued by the prospect of going off travelling with Elaine. But when she had started going on about not coming back to this country and 'inventing new lives' for themselves – well, that had put a different slant on things.

It wasn't only the thought of not seeing his friends and family again that worried him, it was the fact that Elaine seemed to be assuming that they would be spending their lives together – as a couple. It wasn't something Ollie had ever considered before. He and Elaine got on well –

they really did – but he wasn't in love with her. Never had been – hadn't thought about whether he ever would be. That was the bottom line. And that was what bothered him.

He had been surprised by what Elaine had said. He'd always thought she'd felt the same way about him. When they first started seeing each other, she had been the one to press the fact that she was a free spirit. She was always fiercely independent, doing her own thing, going off for weekends with various 'save the planet' groups. Which was fine by Ollie. He was happy to go along with the no-pressure relationship.

That was why it was all the more odd that she should now be talking about their future, of settling down in another country, *together*.

Ollie wasn't sure he was up to taking such a big risk and he would hate the idea of her shelling out for his ticket only for them to fall out half-way round the world. The guilt would be unbearable. And yet she was offering him such a brilliant opportunity. Would he be mad to turn it down?

He was relieved when he heard his mum shouting from downstairs that there was a phone call for him. It meant he could put off thinking about this for a bit longer. He was pleased when he heard Kerry's friendly voice at the other end of the line.

"I was calling to see how you got on with Joe," she explained. "I didn't like to ask back at the river, not when the others were around. Is he OK?"

"To be honest, Kez, I don't know," replied Ollie. "We ran into Catrina on the way home and she had a right go at him."

"Why? What happened?" Kerry sounded puzzled.

"I'm still not sure. She was going on at him to sort his life out, really tearing into him – you know what she can be like with her opinions." Ollie sighed. "Anyway, Joe hit back, told her to get off his case and then stormed off. I haven't seen him since. I knocked on his door when I got back from work this evening but there was no answer."

"I can't believe Cat could be so cruel! Didn't she realise what a state he was in?"

"I think it was seeing how bad he was that got her going," explained Ollie. "It was weird. Then when I tried to get her to explain herself, she flounced off too. It would have cut quite a funny scene if it hadn't been so awful."

"So you didn't manage to get Joe to talk about what's going on then?"

"No, he was too boozed-up to be at all coherent." Ollie sighed again. "And I feel really bad, like I've let him down. This must have been going on for some while for him to look so rough, but I had no idea. And I still don't know what it's all about."

"He's not the easiest person to figure out, though, is he?" Kerry pondered, searching for the right words to make Ollie feel better. "I doubt if anyone knows what's going on inside his head. It must be pretty bad for him to be blocking it out with drink."

"I know. At least now I've got an idea of what's going on, I'll make a point of trying to catch him as soon as I can," Ollie continued. "And if you do the same, we might get somewhere. But I still think we ought to keep this to ourselves, don't you? Cat's a bit of a loose cannon. Maybe one of us could talk to her..."

"I'll give it a go. And try not to worry too much, Ol. Maybe it's just a phase he's going through."

"I hope you're right, 'cause I am pretty worried actually. I never realised he was so low."

"Yeah, I guess he really needs us now. Or at least, he needs *you* in particular," said Kerry. "You're the only one Joe ever talks to, aren't you? I mean, *really* talks to. More than anyone, you'll be the person he's most likely to open up to."

"I only hope I'll be here long enough to see

him through it, that's all," Ollie said, though he hadn't quite meant to voice his thoughts aloud just yet.

"What do you mean?"

"Elaine's going off on a round-the-world trip. And she wants me to go with her."

"You're kidding me!" Kerry was stunned.

"Er, nope. Shocker, eh?"

"So... so what have you said? Are you *going*?"

"Dunno. I'm thinking about it. I said I'd call her in the week."

"When would you be going?"

"In a month or so." Ollie could hardly believe he was talking so rationally about something he was still so up-in-the-air about.

"Oh, Ollie, I don't know what to say. I mean, it's such a great opportunity, but so soon? I can't believe it."

"Neither can I really. I guess I've got a lot of thinking to do in the next day or so."

Kerry came away from the conversation feeling absolutely shell-shocked. With Sonja treating her as if she didn't exist any more and Ollie thinking about leaving Winstead – no, more than that, the country – it felt as if she was losing her two best friends at once.

CHAPTER 15

••••••••••••••••••••••••••••

A BAD DAY FOR KERRY AND JOE

Whenever Kerry was depressed she shopped. And today she was indulging in a huge spending bender in an attempt to cheer herself up. So far, although she was laden down with New Look, Miss Selfridge and HMV bags, and had blown all the money she'd been saving for a new CD player, it wasn't working.

However much she tried, she couldn't get the events of the last few days out of her mind. It had got to the point where she felt she was going around with a permanent frown on her face.

First, there was all this stuff with Sonja. Kerry had deliberately avoided going anywhere near her since the picnic by the river when Sonja had made it blatantly obvious that she didn't want to talk to Kerry.

Even Natasha had looked bemused at one point, as if she was wondering what was going on between the two (former?) best friends.

And Maya had definitely noticed something was up. She had discreetly asked Kerry if she was all right and Kerry had insisted that she was. (The last thing she wanted was the analytical Maya organising an immediate discussion group so that they could thrash out any differences.)

Kerry had come to the conclusion that if she wasn't such a wimp she would have phoned Sonja by now to demand an explanation. But Kerry knew she didn't have the guts to do that, hence the avoidance tactics. And as far as she was concerned, it wasn't up to her to force the issue. Sonja was the one in the wrong here and it was down to her to realise that and make amends.

What made Kerry feel even worse was the nagging suspicion that Sonja didn't miss her at all. You would have thought that it would be hard to forget so many years of friendship, but seeing as Sonja hadn't even bothered to call Kerry recently, it was obvious that their relationship meant less to Sonja than it did to Kerry.

Niggling away in the back of Kerry's mind was the thought that maybe Sonja would follow Natasha to London to become a model. Then what? What chance would their friendship have of surviving such a distance and life-style change? The idea made Kerry even more miserable.

Kerry was also really worried about Joe. In many ways, Kerry identified with him. He was quiet, like her, and he sat on the fringes of the group, rather than being in the thick of it. Kerry felt she was like that, too – an outsider looking in, rather than a fully-fledged gang member.

She understood Joe's shyness and his awkwardness. She tried to imagine what was happening in his life to make him turn to alcohol and was desperate to help him in whatever way she could. It was tragic seeing him looking twice his age, so drawn and haggard, the shy smile replaced by a vacant expression.

And finally, there was the bombshell from Ollie. Kerry had tried to imagine life without Ollie countless times since his news. And each time she got more depressed.

Ollie was by far her closest male friend. The prospect of not seeing his lovely, smiley face, or hearing his cheerful optimism on almost any subject, didn't bear thinking about. She would even miss hearing him singing or playing sax in The Loud when they practised at the back of The Swan, which showed how much she cared about Ollie as they often weren't very good.

Kerry didn't think she'd ever meet another guy

like Ollie. She sometimes felt they were soul mates, though she'd never admitted *that* to anyone.

Losing him would be like losing a limb.

Kerry traipsed around the Plaza shopping centre for a while longer, her mood deteriorating with every step. Then, just as she was rounding a corner to go into What She Wants, she caught sight of Sonja and Natasha.

Arms linked, laden down with bags from trendy shops, they were strolling along and laughing together, as if they'd been best friends for ever. It was just too much for Kerry to bear. She turned on her heel and began hurrying the other way.

But the sudden flurry of movement caught Sonja's eye and she spotted Kerry hotfooting it in the opposite direction.

"Hey, Kez!" she called out.

Kerry ignored her. She wasn't going to let Sonja Harvey see the tears streaming down her face.

• • •

Joe felt much better than he had for quite some time. He put this down to the fact that he hadn't touched a drink for a couple of days. Not since Catrina had so bluntly brought it home to him just how bad he looked. That and the fact that he'd felt ten times worse on the inside had brought him to his senses.

Once he'd made a conscious decision to lay off the booze, the combination of resolve, self-will and not going anywhere near Henry's had helped him along the way. The knowledge that he hadn't found it too difficult to abstain convinced him that he was by no means an alcoholic and that he could turn this phase in his life round, if he was determined enough.

But it was like walking on shards of glass. A painful mental tussle of epic proportions continually fought itself out in his head. As long as he remained hopeful about himself and his life, he was OK. But as soon as he let any doubt in, he could almost see the invisible wall of optimism he had built begin to crumble.

For a person who always saw the glass as half empty rather than half full, retaining a positive outlook was no mean feat. Joe was managing it so far by having little projects to look forward to. Ollie had mentioned The Loud playing a gig in a month or so which Joe was hugely enthusiastic about.

He had even started writing a new song for Ollie to sing. It was a smoochy ballad, something he hadn't tackled before, and it was all about

Kerry. One day he would sing it to her himself, when he knew she felt the same way about him.

He was whistling the chorus of Kerry's song and walking towards Nick's Slick Riffs where he thought he might catch up with Ollie, when he saw Kerry coming towards him.

This is fate, Joe thought. His face broke into an involuntary smile as he watched her rushing up the street, bags of shopping weighing her down. And his stomach flipped excitedly when she noticed him too and gave him a big smile.

"Hello, Joe," she said warmly. "That's funny, I was only thinking about you a few moments ago."

'Wh-what?" Joe could hardly believe what he was hearing. Kerry was thinking about *him*? Wow!

"Yeah," she continued, unaware of the effect those few words had on his heartbeat. "I was wondering how you were. Y'know, after... the other day."

"Oh, yeah, *that*," Joe said, a little disheartened. He didn't need reminding of Sunday; it had been the real low point in his life so far.

To be caught red-handed in a drunken stupor by the two people he cared about most was pretty humiliating.

It had been another reason for quitting that scene.

"Yeah, I, uh... I'm really sorry, Kerry. You know, that you had to see me like that. I was pretty out of it."

"You look heaps better now though, almost back to your old self."

This was in fact a lie. Joe still looked pretty rough, but Kerry guessed he didn't need to hear that right now. At least he seemed capable of stringing a sentence together.

"I guess I've been letting things get on top of me recently. Kind of went off the rails for a while." Joe raised his eyebrows and gave her a shy smile, which Kerry found rather touching.

"We had no idea, Joe. Are you OK now, though?" Kerry wasn't going to push the subject – if Joe wanted to confide in her that was great; if not, well that was his business.

"Back on track, I guess," he replied, scuffing the toe of his DM on the concrete paving slab he was studying. He wasn't ready to spill his guts to Kerry. He figured it would be a long time before he could do that.

"Good, great," she went on. "Where are you off to now?"

"I was going to look in on Ollie. We've got a gig coming up and I wanted to go through a few things with him – y'know, rehearsals and things."

"So what do you think about Ollie's news?" she asked, forcing a smile.

Joe looked at her blankly. "Huh? Sorry?"

"It's so exciting, isn't it? Going off around the world, not knowing which country you'll be sleeping in next," babbled Kerry, disguising the pain she was feeling with false enthusiasm. "It'll be such a great experience for him and Elaine. I'm dead envious."

"What? What are you talking about?"

Kerry watched Joe's face crumple in front of her. Then the penny dropped. *He didn't know.*

"Oh, Joe, I'm sorry! I thought Ollie must have told you," Kerry spluttered, realising that she'd stuck her foot in it. "I, uh, guess he hasn't yet." She didn't know what else to say.

"Uh, no, I... guess not," Joe replied slowly. He was devastated by this information.

Ollie was going travelling with Elaine? Leaving Winstead? For how long – months, years? And Ollie hadn't even bothered to tell him. Why? Didn't Ollie consider him a worthy enough friend any more? Didn't he care? Did *anyone* care?

Kerry's mind was racing too. Why hadn't Ollie told Joe? Then she remembered Ollie saying he hadn't seen Joe, how he'd knocked on his door the other evening after work, but Joe hadn't been there. They obviously hadn't seen each other since.

Kerry opened her mouth to speak, but Joe was already half-way down the road.

"Joe? Joe!" Kerry called after him.

Joe didn't answer. He started to run. Away from Kerry. Away from Ollie. Away from this dull, stupid, *worthless* life.

CHAPTER 16

● ●

FROM BAD TO WORSE

"So he just *ran off*?"

"Yep, he didn't say goodbye or anything. And he looked so hurt. I'm really sorry, Ollie. I didn't know you hadn't seen him. I just assumed everyone knew by now."

Kerry and Ollie were huddled in a corner of the End-of-the-Line café, away from Catrina, Matt and Maya, who were sitting at their usual table by the big bay window. Kerry was so mortified about telling Joe Ollie's news before Ollie had had a chance to that she'd immediately gone to look for him to confess.

"I think Joe was the only one who didn't know," Ollie replied. "Basically because he's never been there when I've called on him. Or at least if he has, then he hasn't answered the door."

Ollie registered the look of anguish on Kerry's face and tried to think of something to say to make her feel better. "It's not your fault, Kerry – you weren't to know. I just wish he wasn't being so elusive at the moment. He isn't in any of the places you'd usually expect to find him. The band are rehearsing tomorrow night. I only hope he turns up."

"Oh, I'm sure he will." Kerry brightened up at the thought. "Joe wouldn't miss a rehearsal for the world."

"I know. They only happen once in a blue moon and he's the keenest of the lot, so we'll have to wait and see." Ollie's expression changed. "Oh, and I caught Cat on her own earlier and warned her not to say anything to anyone."

"And?"

"And she said she had no intention of mentioning it. She was hoping to see Joe to apologise. Can you believe that?"

"What? Cat apologise? Wonders never cease! It's not like her to back down – she must feel really bad."

The pair broke off from their whispering as they spotted Anna coming back from the kitchen with Kerry's order of fries for the group.

"Hey, Ollie, why don't you knock off for the night?" said Anna brightly. "I'll finish up here.

There's not much left to do and I don't suppose anyone else'll come in now."

"Really, Anna? That's great. Cheers."

Ollie whipped his blue and white striped pinny off and took the tray of food over to the others.

"So, Ol, have you decided whether or not you're buggering off round the world yet?" drawled Matt.

"Nah, not yet. I've still got a lot of thinking to do."

"Christ, what is there to think about?" Catrina rasped. "I'd be off like a shot."

"Yeah, me too." Matt added.

I wish it was as simple as that, Ollie thought. He hadn't told anyone that Elaine had talked about never coming home. He thought it would be better if he kept that bit to himself.

"Well, I'd have to think long and hard," Maya countered. "I'd really miss my family and friends."

"Yeah, but Ollie doesn't have that problem," Cat piped up. "He hasn't got any friends."

Ollie was stopped from having to think of a bitchy reply by the *ping!* of the doorbell as Sonja came into the café.

"Hi guys," she said brightly. "I thought I might find you lot here."

"Hello stranger," Matt replied. "Where's your sidekick?"

"Huh? Oh, you mean Tasha! She's gone back to London. I've just been to the station actually. I gave her a hand with her luggage and stuff."

Sonja slumped on to the long seat next to Matt. "I thought I'd invite her back down for your party next weekend, Matt."

"You'll have a job," Ollie countered. "She goes to Japan on Wednesday."

"Wh-what do you mean?" asked Sonja, perplexed.

"She's off to Japan to work. She won't be back for weeks."

"Oh!" Sonja was clearly taken aback. "So how come she didn't mention that to me?"

"Search me," Ollie said. "She probably never thought about it."

"Oh. Right," Sonja said in a distinctly huffy tone. "Well, that's nice, isn't it? There's me, going out of my way to make her feel welcome round here, and she doesn't have the decency to tell me she's not going to be back in Winstead for ages. She could have at least told me. I thought we were friends."

Kerry was staggered by what she was hearing. The cheek of it, after all that Sonja had put her through recently! How shallow could she get? Kerry could feel the anger bubbling inside her. Very soon she was going to blow her top and tell

Sonja exactly what she thought of her.

Kerry began counting to ten... very slowly.

As she got to six Sonja was still waffling on about how hurt she was by 'Natasha's' (funny how she had suddenly become Natasha again) apparent oversight, especially when Sonja had planned so many things for them to do in the coming months. By the time she'd counted to nine, Kerry was livid.

She stood up, heaved an exaggerated sigh and announced to anyone who wasn't listening to Sonja prattle on, that she was leaving.

This stopped the conversation dead in its tracks.

"What?" Maya exclaimed. "But you haven't finished your fries."

"I know." Kerry spoke through gritted teeth. "But if I stay any longer I might say something I regret. I'll see you around."

Kerry slid out of the banquette and headed for the door. Leaving a sea of baffled faces behind her, she stumbled out into the street and fled.

"What's up with *her*?" asked Sonja archly.

"Come on, Sonja, wake up. What do you *think* that was about?" Ollie looked at her in sheer astonishment.

"Huh? *I* dunno. You tell me."

"OK, I will. You've been an absolute cow

to Kerry ever since Natasha came home. You've been acting like she didn't exist."

"What? What are you talking about?" Sonja seemed genuinely surprised by Ollie's outburst.

Ollie shook his head in disbelief. She really didn't have a clue.

"You've spent practically every waking hour with Natasha and hardly said a word to Kez the whole time my bloody sister's been around."

"I have *not*," Sonja said, indignantly. "Kerry's been out with us! We went to that dreadful club the other night."

"Yeah and that's about the only place you *have* been with her," snorted Ollie. "The rest of the time you've ignored her. At one point Kerry thought she must have done something to upset you. Like it was *her* fault."

"Well, if that's all the thanks I get for looking after your sister, I won't bother in future," said Sonja snottily.

"My sister is quite capable of looking after herself," Ollie replied.

"Ollie's right. You have been ignoring Kerry recently," Maya joined in. "I've noticed it myself."

"Oh, so you mean she's been bitching about me behind my back rather than saying anything to my face. I see." Sonja was even more indignant now.

"No, that's not it at all," Maya carried on calmly. "Kerry hasn't said a word to me – she didn't need to – I worked it out for myself. Face facts, Son, you have been a little wrapped up in Natasha at the expense of your friendship with Kerry. Don't you see it?"

"Yeah, I've noticed it too," Catrina added, although she hadn't noticed it at all.

"Oh, for God's sake, don't *you* start!" Sonja snapped, her bottom lip quivering. "I'm not staying here to be picked on by you lot. I'm going home."

Sonja shoved her way out of her seat and stomped out of the café.

Smirking, Catrina lit a cigarette. "What a thrilling evening's entertainment," she said dryly. "I wonder who's next for the dramatic exit?"

CHAPTER 17

● ●

OLLIE MAKES UP HIS MIND

Kerry tapped gingerly on the back door of The Swan, not quite sure what she was doing there, but feeling as if she needed to see a friendly face. She was embarrassed by her outburst at the End and wanted to sound Ollie out to see what sort of reaction her rapid exit had caused.

When Ollie's mum answered the door, she told Kerry to go upstairs to the living room where, she said, he was on the phone.

Kerry heard Ollie speaking as she approached the room from the long hallway.

"...I know, but it just wouldn't feel right," he was saying gently. "I couldn't go with you unless I was absolutely sure, and I'm not."

There was silence as the person he was speaking to took up the conversation.

Then Kerry heard Ollie's voice once again.

"I'm really sorry, E. I just can't do it. It is a brilliant opportunity, I realise that, but I've made up my mind. I'm so sorry."

Kerry was acutely embarrassed as she realised she was overhearing Ollie talking to Elaine, and it was quite apparent what they were talking about.

"Yeah," Ollie went on. "Do. Send me a postcard or two, won't you? And I am envious of you; it's just not the right time for me to go. Let's meet up before you go to say goodbye..."

Kerry thought about turning round and scarpering, but at that moment Ollie looked towards the door and saw her hovering in the corridor. He smiled and beckoned to her to come in. Moments later, he put the phone down.

"I'm so sorry," Kerry spluttered. "I didn't realise you were on the phone – your mum sent me straight up. I, uh, overheard..."

"That's OK, Kez, I was going to call you as soon as I'd spoken to E anyway."

"So you're not going then?"

"No. It was tempting, but, well, I've got too much to lose around here, haven't I?"

"You have? Like what?" Kerry asked, frowning slightly.

Ollie ran his fingers through his hair, pulling it back from his face and exposing his boyish features. "Well, uh, you know. Friends. You. I, uh, I'd miss the conversations we have, you know?"

Kerry came over and gave Ollie a friendly hug. "I'm so pleased, Ol," she said. "I was hoping you'd stay. I'd miss you, too."

"Geez, thanks," Ollie replied, bashful for once in his life. He quickly changed the subject, filling Kerry in on events after she'd left the café, right down to Sonja's quivering lip routine as she too flounced off.

Kerry felt even worse.

"So," he continued, "has Sonja contacted you yet to say sorry?"

Kerry shrugged her shoulders. "No, she hasn't. I guess she doesn't think she owes me an apology. I feel really silly about the way I stormed out. I can just imagine what the others were saying."

"Don't," Ollie scolded. "Don't feel guilty. Just remember that Sonja's made your life hell and she's the one who owes *you* an apology. She'll come round. Trust me."

Kerry nodded and smiled feebly.

"I was gonna call on Joe again," Ollie continued. "To remind him about the rehearsal. Why don't you come too?"

"Sure." Kerry had intended seeing Joe to make amends for her gaffe in the street yesterday.

Having Ollie there as back-up would make the task easier.

They made their way outside and crossed the street to where Joe lived in a little terraced house with his mum. Ollie tapped on the door.

No answer. He banged the door with his fist. Still no reply.

"I'm getting used to this... I feel like I'm better friends with this door than I am with Joe these days," said Ollie wryly.

"What about his mum? Wasn't she in at all?"

"Only once. She said he'd told her he was going out with Matt that time, which I know wasn't true."

"Did she seem worried about him?"

"She did ask me a lot more questions than usual, like whether I'd seen much of Joe, whether I knew how things were at college, whether he seemed OK to me. I didn't like to put the frighteners on her so I played dumb. Y'know, 'Oh everything's fine, Mrs Gladwin'."

"Hmmm, I guess that's the best way or Joe'll have her breathing down his neck," nodded Kerry sympathetically. "I can't imagine that would help much. Let's just hope you see him tonight to get an idea of how he really is."

"Uh-huh. Are you coming?" Ollie asked. "We could do with an independent opinion."

"Sure, I'd love to." Kerry smiled. "Beats sitting in front of the telly all night."

"Great. Well, I'd better head off for another hard shift at the office. I'll see you later on."

"Yeah, and I really am pleased that you're staying, Ollie. Winstead wouldn't be the same without you."

Giving her his broadest grin and a cheery wave, Ollie turned and headed to the café. And Kerry set off back home a lot happier than when she'd left that morning. Maybe now that one part of her life was on the up, the rest would improve too.

• • •

The sound of thrashing guitars and Ollie's straining vocals coming from the room at the back of The Swan was pretty deafening, Kerry thought, as she walked up to the door and tugged it open.

Inside on the low stage at the front of the room were three members of The Loud: Ollie (singer/songwriter/sax), Mick (guitar) and Rob (bass). There was no sign of Joe on drums, and even Kerry with her untrained ear could tell that the balance was all wrong.

Sitting at a table at the far side of the stage was Cat and Mick's new girlfriend/Barbie doll, Ally.

Kerry didn't feel the slightest tinge of envy seeing her there, which made her realise that she was completely over fancying Mick.

Cat and Ally didn't appear to be paying much attention to the band, as they chain-smoked cigarettes and shouted at each other in an attempt to be heard above the din.

Kerry went over to join them, glancing at Ollie as she passed the stage. His face was scrunched up in a grimace as he sang and he looked really hacked off. This rehearsal obviously wasn't going at all well.

The song ended and Ollie jumped offstage and walked over to the girls.

"I don't suppose you play drums, do you, Kez?" he said grimly.

"He's not turned up yet then?" Kerry asked rather obviously.

Ollie shook his head and took a gulp of orange juice from a pint glass. "We couldn't wait any longer, but it sounds crap without drums."

"It doesn't usually sound too good with them," joked Catrina. Then, referring to the time she had wowed the crowd with an amazing Catwoman performance at a Loud gig, added, "Would you like me to come in and save the day for you again?"

"Shut up, Cat," Ollie said irritably.

Just then the door crashed open and someone barged into the room.

It was Joe.

Ollie was delighted. "Great to see you, mate. We're the pits without you!" he beamed.

But his smile faded as he saw his friend storming towards him with a look of pure fury on his face.

"Why didn't you tell me?" Joe screamed, his hands clenched into tight, white-knuckled fists.

"What?"

"The least you could have done was tell me yourself," Joe continued, his face inches from Ollie's, his pupils so dilated it was impossible to see the natural colour of his eyes.

At once Ollie worked out what Joe was on about.

"Joe, I'm really sorry. I've been trying to catch you since..."

"Cut the crap, Ollie," Joe spat, cutting him off mid-sentence. "I trusted you. I thought we were friends..."

"We are, Joe," Ollie tried to reason. But Joe wasn't listening.

"Well, you know what you can do?" he continued, swaying slightly as he spoke. "You can stuff your friendship and stuff your stupid band. I can do without friends like you."

Joe turned around and headed for the door. Ollie made to go after him.

"No, Ollie, let me go." Catrina got up quickly from her chair.

"You?" Kerry spluttered incredulously. "Why would he listen to you of all people?"

"Trust me," Catrina said briskly over her shoulder. "I know what I'm doing."

Ollie stood back and let her pass.

"*Ollie?*" Kerry cried, looking at him as if he was barmy. "What's happening?"

"It's OK, Kerry. Leave her."

Kerry watched open-mouthed as Catrina disappeared out of the door. *What the hell was going on?*

CHAPTER 18

• •

CAT COMES CLEAN

Catrina found Joe sitting on a wooden bench a little way down the road from the pub. She sat down at the other end of the seat. Joe didn't move, didn't turn to see who it was. He just stared into the last of the evening sunlight, wrapped up in his own thoughts.

Catrina knew what she wanted to say – she had it all planned out. The question was, would Joe listen or would he tell her to get lost?

There was only one way to find out. Cat took out her cigarettes, lit one up, then spoke.

"I'm not going to sit here and lecture you, Joe, but I know what you've been up to and I guess I want to help..."

"Oh, *yeah*? And why would *you* of all people want to do that?" Joe muttered angrily.

"Well, because I've seen it all before. And I've seen what booze can do to someone. And believe me, it's not nice to watch someone fall apart because of it."

"And what makes you think I'm falling apart?"

"Come on, Joe, it's obvious to anyone who knows you that you've been acting pretty strange recently. I– I needed to say something before it's too late."

"Why? What do *you* care?" Joe's voice was hard, and he didn't let himself look at Catrina.

"I don't want to watch you go the same way as I've seen other drunks go, namely into the gutter…"

"And since when have you been such an expert on the subject?" Joe sneered. "What do you know about it?"

Catrina drew on her cigarette and thought for a moment, struggling to find a way to say what she knew Joe had to hear. Finally, she took a deep breath and spoke.

"I know plenty actually. I lost my dad to alcohol."

Joe turned to look at Catrina. He stared at her intently for what seemed like ages. His brain was trying to remember what he knew of Catrina's family.

As far as he could remember, her dad had run off a few years ago. That meant Cat was lying and not for the first time. Joe gave her a scornful look.

"No you *didn't,*" he scoffed. "He left you.

Dumped on you and your mum and scarpered."

"Yeah, well that's what we tell everyone," Cat said wearily. "No one knows the truth 'cause Mum can't bear for anyone to know what really happened."

"And what about you?"

"Well, how d'you think you'd feel if your father'd sold all the furniture in the house to buy drink? How he'd lost his job, car, how he defaulted on the mortgage, stopped paying bills? All because he liked booze more than anything else."

Joe searched Catrina's eyes, trying to work out whether she was telling the truth. If she wasn't, she was doing a pretty good job of lying. Her eyes were full of tears and her voice wobbled as she spoke.

"So you lied about it?" he asked.

"Yep." Catrina paused to light up another cigarette. "It was Mum's idea. She tried to pretend everything was normal. She used to make excuses for people not to come to the house 'cause there was nothing in it. Crazy really..."

"So no one knew?"

"Only Sonja's mum and dad and they've been sworn to secrecy. I don't think even Sonja knows the whole truth. Mum was too proud to ask for help. She would never have let on to anyone that we were in such a mess." Cat gave a watery smile. "She's always been a high achiever; she wouldn't admit what a state things were in. She thought she could handle Dad without professional help. You know, get him off the booze."

"So what happened?"

"Well, Dad came to the conclusion that he preferred alcohol to his wife and daughter..." Catrina broke off, tears sliding down her heavily made-up cheeks. "And when... when Mum gave him an ultimatum, like g-get straight or get out, well, he got out."

"What, left you?"

"Yep. Didn't even say g-g-goodbye. That's how much he thought of me."

"But why did he leave? Why didn't he stay and try and straighten himself out?"

"I guess because he didn't w-w-want to. He wanted booze more than he wanted his family."

"Cat, I had no idea..." Joe's voice cracked. "I'm so sorry. Do you know where he is now?"

"Absolutely no idea. He's never contacted us, never sent a card at Christmas or on my birthday. He could be dead for all I know."

They sat in silence for some time, Catrina relieved that she'd finally told someone the secret that had been eating away at her for years.

Joe contemplated what she'd said, trying to relate it to his own situation. He couldn't quite work that bit out.

"Why did you tell me this?" he asked finally.

"I would have thought that was obvious," Catrina replied quietly.

"You mean you think I'm going to end up like your dad? What do you think I am, stupid or something?"

"Well, you must be to be drinking so much in the first place," Catrina snapped, sounding more like her usual self. "Come on, Joe, get real. You might think you've got a long way to go to end up like my dad. That it'll never happen to you. But if you don't sort yourself out now, before you know it you'll be out there with him. I'd put money on it. I bet you've already thought about nicking off your mum or selling something to pay for a cheap bottle of vodka."

Joe didn't answer – the look on his face said it all. He had already stolen twenty quid from his mum's purse. That was last week. How much longer before he sold his Sony Walkman, his CD collection, just so he could get wasted on drink?

"That won't happen to me," Joe said a little too feebly for Catrina's liking.

"That's what they all say," she snorted derisively. "According to Mum, Dad thought he was on top of it throughout, even when we had the bailiffs knocking on the door. Dad justified it right up until the day he left."

Catrina stopped and took a deep breath. "Look," she said more gently, "it's up to you. You might think you're only messing around, and you can stop whenever you want, but you're kidding yourself. That's how Dad was. He never realised it controlled him, or at least he never admitted it."

"I'm amazed that you've never told anyone before," Joe said.

"Well I wouldn't have told you if it hadn't been necessary," replied Cat. "And I'd appreciate it if you'd keep it to yourself. I don't want anyone else to know. OK? Mum will go mad if she ever finds out that I've told you."

"Sure. But... but would you do the same for me, please? You know, not tell anyone about this either?"

"Yep, that's a deal."

"And thanks," Joe added simply.

● ● ●

Kerry lay on her bed listening to the dance compilation she'd bought on her shopping binge and completing a magazine quiz called Best Friend Or Worst Enemy? Relating every question to her relationship with Sonja, with only three points scored so far, the outlook for their friendship looked bleak.

Her mother saved her from sinking into further depression by tapping on her door and saying there was a phone call for her. Still holding the magazine, Kerry left her room, went downstairs, picked up the phone and said hello.

"Hi," Sonja's voice said brightly. "How's things?"

Kerry was gobsmacked. Talk about spooky! She hadn't expected to hear from *her* at all. What was back-from-the-dead Sonja doing calling her up out of the blue like this?

"Fine," Kerry answered in a flat voice. She certainly wasn't going to make this too easy for Sonja. Her 'friend' was going to have to explain her recent actions before Kerry gave her the time of day.

"I just wondered if you wanted to come and see that new Matt Damon film with me. We could go for a pizza before, if you like."

Kerry seethed. It was apparent from the tone of the conversation that Sonja had no intention of offering any kind of apology. Who the heck did she think she was calling up and pretending nothing had happened?

Kerry didn't bother counting to ten as usual; it was time that Sonja heard exactly how she felt.

"You must be joking!" she barked into the phone. "Do you really think I'm gonna want to hang out with you after the way you've been acting? You must think I'm really dumb!"

"Sorry?" Sonja said, startled.

"I suppose you think that now your new friend has buggered off to Japan, you can pick up the pieces with me, do you? You're thinking, *Good old Kerry, she's always around to hang out with.* And I suppose you reckoned I'd be grateful for this call, did you?"

"Kerry, don't you think you're over-reacting a bit here?" Sonja said pointedly. "It's not as if I've been ignoring you..."

"Are you kidding?" Kerry exclaimed. "That's exactly what you *have* been doing! Ever since you hooked up with Natasha, it's been like I don't exist any more."

"I think you're being a little oversensitive—"

"And aren't you being totally *insensitive*?" Kerry raged. "Come on Sonja, think about it – just for once in your life. How would you feel if your so-called best friend had hardly said a word to you for days, let alone included you in her social diary?"

"C'mon Kerry, you're exaggerating. We went to Henry's together, and that picnic by the river—"

"Where you spent the entire afternoon whispering to Natasha and ignoring me!"

"I hate to say this Kerry, but you're being just a bit neurotic—"

"And you're being a selfish, narrow-minded, two-faced cow!"

Kerry slammed the phone down and hurled her magazine at the nearest wall.

CHAPTER 19

• •

THE PENNY DROPS

Click! Brrrr...

Sonja stared at the phone for a few seconds, unable to believe that Kerry would hang up on her. But she had.

God, she must be really mad at me to do that! Sonja thought. *I had no idea...*

Sonja lay on the bed and retraced her life in the last week or so. Then she picked up the phone again, punching in Maya's number.

"Hello?"

"Hello, Maya? It's Sonja. What are you up to?"

"Hi, Son, uh – nothing much. Waiting for *Home and Away* to come on."

"You don't fancy meeting me for a pizza tonight, do you?"

"Uh, difficult one. I'm not sure I'll be able to

get away. You don't fancy coming round here, do you?"

"Sure."

"Is everything OK? You sound a bit down."

"Yeah everything's fine. Kind of. I, uh, I'll explain when I see you. Is half-seven OK?"

"Fine. I'll see you then."

"Yep. Bye."

Sonja put the phone down and lay on her bed for the next hour. Thinking.

● ● ●

Sonja stared bleakly at her coffee mug and wiped her nose again with her hanky. Her eyes and nose were red from the combination of crying and being constantly rubbed. She had been on the verge of tears ever since she'd spoken to Maya earlier. Since then she'd had time to reflect on what she'd done and the guilt was weighing heavily on her. She had barely got through the door before she had begun pouring her heart out to Maya.

"So then she told me what she thought of me..." *(sniff)*

"Uh huh."

"And then she slammed the phone down on me."

"Oh."

"And now I feel... *(sniff)* terrible."

Sonja looked up at Maya who gave her a little smile of sympathy.

"So, what do I do?" she continued. "D'you think I've blown it?"

"*Nooo*, I don't think that at all," Maya said, choosing her words carefully. "But, as I think I said to you in the café, maybe you got a little too wrapped up in Natasha. This row has been on the cards for a while now, hasn't it?"

"Uh, I guess so," Sonja said. "I just didn't see it, that's all."

"So you agree that maybe Kerry has a point?"

"Yeah. But the thing I don't understand is why she never said anything to me before?"

"That's not really Kerry's style, is it? She's the sort who'll put up with a lot of crap before she lets it get to her. And knowing Kerry, she probably started off wondering whether *she'd* done something wrong."

"Yeah, you're probably right. So you think I've given her 'a lot of crap', do you?"

"Mmm," Maya said pointedly between gulps of coffee. "I do and I reckon you know that too, if you're being really honest."

"But I didn't mean to," wailed Sonja. "Surely you believe that?"

"Of course I do and I expect Kerry does too.

But that doesn't let you off the hook, does it? You should have thought about her feelings more than you did."

"I know. I've been such a thoughtless cow, I feel really bad about it." Sonja's chin began to wobble as she spoke and her eyes filled with tears again. "I honestly didn't think the thing with Natasha was causing any friction with Kez. I thought she *liked* her..."

"I think she did, Son," Maya sighed. "That's not what the problem was. It was the fact that you became so cliquey with her that you pushed Kerry's nose out of joint."

"And then I put my foot in it big time, as soon as Tasha left, by trying to carry on as though nothing had happened," nodded Sonja, as she played it over in her mind.

"Kind of the icing on the cake for Kerry."

"How could I have been so stupid?" Sonja held her head in her hands and stared at the pattern on Maya's bedroom carpet. She racked her brains. "So what do I do now? I mean, she won't even speak to me. How can I apologise if she won't even see me?"

Maya thought for a moment. "Well, if it was me I'd leave it for a day to let her calm down a bit. In fact, I'd leave it until Matt's party tomorrow night. That's the best thing. She's bound to be there and she certainly won't want to make a scene in front of everyone – Kerry would hate that – so maybe you could make peace with her then."

"But what if she won't forgive me?" Sonja howled. "What do I do then? I'll have lost my absolute best friend and it'll all be my fault."

"That won't happen. Kerry's a reasonable person," Maya said confidently. "Believe me, she'll come round. So long as you eat plenty of humble pie and don't get on your high horse like you did in the café the other night. Do *that* and you really will blow it."

Sonja nodded her agreement and prayed that for once in her life she might be able to keep her big mouth shut.

CHAPTER 20

●●●●●●●●●●●●●●●●●●●●●●●●●●

NOTHING BUT THE TRUCE

Kerry could hear the Beastie Boys blaring out as she walked down the lane to Matt's house. Matt's parties were always a laugh, and tonight's should be especially good as his dad had gone to stay with a friend.

Not that *that* was so unusual. Kerry was always very envious of the free rein Matt seemed to have. She couldn't imagine *her* parents letting her keep the entire neighbourhood awake, as the thumping bass of Matt's sound system threatened to do.

In the past she would have arranged to meet Sonja beforehand, but seeing as that wasn't likely to happen any more, this was one party Kerry didn't mind walking into on her own.

As soon as she'd squeezed past the couple

snogging at the front door, she saw loads of faces she knew.

She headed for the kitchen, but seeing Sonja in there gassing to someone from college, she turned tail and dashed down into Matt's basement instead.

"Hi, Kez, good to see you!" Ollie yelled above the din, tapping Kerry's arm as she walked past and motioning her towards him.

"Oh hi, Ollie. Been here long?"

"About half an hour. It's a good party though, isn't it?"

Kerry nodded.

"And look over there..." Ollie pointed towards the other side of the room where Catrina seemed to be in deep conversation with Joe. "They've been standing there talking like that for about twenty minutes."

"Really?" Kerry said, surprised. "I wonder what about? I don't think Joe's ever had more than three words to say to Cat in his entire life before now."

"I know. And doesn't Joe look better?"

"Yeah, much. He's lost that walking-dead look. Have you seen him since he got mad at you the other night?"

"No, I was hoping to have a word here, but he hasn't left Cat's side at all yet. And I'm not keen on butting in in case I'm interrupting something, you know?"

"What do you mean?" Kerry asked.

Then her eyes widened as she took in Ollie's expression. "What, you mean you think there's something going on between them?"

"Who knows?" Ollie shrugged. "But they look very close, don't you think?"

"Well, yeah, I suppose so. But Joe and Cat? Having a thing going? Surely not!"

"Stranger things have happened."

"Yeah," Kerry sniggered, her eyes twinkling mischievously. "I seem to remember you and Cat being, er, quite close not too long ago. And if that wasn't an oddball combination, I don't know what is."

"OK, OK, don't rub it in," replied Ollie bashfully. "Look, will you go and grab Cat's attention so that I can speak to Joe? I'd really like to get things sorted between us."

"Sure."

Kerry began weaving in and out of countless bodies grooving furiously on the dance floor as she made her way across the room. Ollie followed behind.

"Joe! Cat! Hi," she yelled as she got close to them. "Great party! Cat, you look fabulous, really good. I love that top! Where did you get it from?"

Chuffed to bits by the compliment, Catrina turned away from Joe and launched into great detail about how she'd tracked it down from a picture in a magazine.

In the meantime, Ollie was able to sidle up to Joe.

"Hello mate, how you doin'?" he asked tentatively.

"Ollie, hi, great to see you," Joe grinned, stepping forward and giving Ollie a bear hug.

"I wasn't sure what kind of reception I was gonna get," Ollie beamed, returning the hug. "Y'know after the other night? I thought you might punch my lights out or something."

"I'm sorry about that, I was in a bit of a state," Joe replied, smiling wanly. "I over-reacted."

"It's OK, mate. I understand," nodded Ollie, pulling a face. "I should've told you about the trip before anyone else – it's just that you hadn't been around much. I did try and find you loads of times."

"Yeah, I know. Really, it's OK. I just got a bit uptight about it – it was irrational really... Anyway, I hear you've decided to stay. Is that right?"

"Yeah," Ollie nodded. "I came to the conclusion that I'd miss everyone around here too much."

"I'm really pleased, Ol. I'd have been gutted if you'd left."

"Aw, shucks," Ollie replied, unable to accept

the compliment unless he took the mick. "And it's good to see you looking heaps better too."

"Yeah, I feel better. I, uh, haven't touched anything for nearly a week – since I balled you out at rehearsals actually."

Joe looked suddenly sheepish. "I'm so ashamed about that, Ol. It really brought me to my senses, you know, that I wasn't fully in control of what I was doing. I had no idea I was gonna blow up at you like that right until I saw you. Then I just snapped – it was scary. I never want to be out of control like that again."

Ollie paused before replying. "I have to admit I was worried about you for a while. If it hadn't been for Cat, I don't know what would have happened."

Joe looked down at the floor, unsure for a moment how much to say about the conversation he'd had with Cat.

He decided it was best to say as little as possible.

"Yeah, Cat was great. She, uh, really talked some sense into me. Made me realise how dumb I was being."

"*Sooo*, does this show you that you *can* talk to girls after all? That maybe they're not creatures from another planet?" Ollie asked, a cheeky look on his face.

Joe laughed. "Uh, yeah, I hadn't thought of that actually. I guess it does. Well, Cat anyway."

"Steady, Joe, you'll be getting a thing about her if you're not careful," Ollie probed. "Or maybe she's getting a thing about you?"

"Oh my God, you don't think that, do you?" Joe gasped, the look of shock on his face immediately telling Ollie that his suspicions were unfounded. "Crikey, Ol, she'd devour me and still have room left for a football team!"

"Just checking," Ollie laughed.

"No," Joe went on. "I guess I've just found out that we've got a lot more in common that I first thought. Cat's OK. She goes a lot deeper than anyone gives her credit for."

Catching sight of Catrina shimmying on the dance floor, her breasts pushed together so that they were under her chin, and surrounded by four guys with their eyes on stalks, Ollie decided that he'd have to take Joe's word for it.

● ● ●

"Kerry? Kerry!"

Sonja pushed her way through the melée of bodies towards Kerry's back which she'd just seen heading up the stairs.

As Kerry reached the top she realised someone

was calling her and looked around. Sonja's face loomed up out of the semi-darkness until they were face to face.

"Oh," Kerry said. "It's you." She made to turn around again and head for the loo, but the desperation in Sonja's voice stalled her.

"Kerry, *please*. You've got to hear me out."

Kerry turned back to face Sonja. "OK, go ahead."

I'm not going to make this easy for you, she thought as she folded her arms across her chest and waited for an explanation.

Sonja gulped before taking a deep breath. "I'm really sorry for what I've put you through. I've been so selfish – a thoughtless old bag who truly doesn't deserve your friendship. I can't begin to tell you how bad I feel about it."

"So why are you telling me this now?" Kerry asked. "Why has it taken until now for you to realise what's been going on?"

"Honestly, Kez," Sonja said, her voice wavering as she spoke. "I had no idea I was being such a cow. Which makes me an even lesser human being for not realising. I don't have any excuses. Not one."

"You're right."

"I know and I'm sorry. I guess I got all wrapped up in having a good time with Natasha and I didn't consider you and your feelings." Sonja paused to take in a nervous gulp of air.

"You know what I'm like, Kez. I'm a nightmare. And when she said all that stuff about me being a model, I was so flattered that someone who lives such a groovy life in London would want to hang out with me, it kind of made me lose sight of who my real friend was."

Sonja looked Kerry directly in the eyes and added, "I only hope that you can forgive me."

Kerry watched two big tears slide down Sonja's cheeks. To hear her apologise was pretty rare – to see her cry was an even more uncommon sight. Kerry suddenly felt hugely and intensely moved.

"It's OK," Kerry's voice wobbled, her eyes welling. "R-really it is."

"Does that m-m-mean we're f-f-friends again?" said Sonja, the tears flowing freely now.

"Course it d-does."

Maya came out of the loo and walked past Kerry and Sonja hugging. She smiled to herself. After all the tension that had been going on recently, it was nice to see that things were getting back to normal.

● ● ●

Joe had never asked a girl to dance before. The fact that he was doing it now, and the fact that he was having the guts to ask the only person in the world he'd *ever* want to dance with, was a huge step forward.

He tapped her on the shoulder.

"Would you like to dance?"

Kerry turned round. "Joe! Hi. Yeah, I'd love to!"

When she smiled and said yes, it felt as good as if she'd agreed to marry Joe. OK, so it might only be a dance – three minutes that probably meant nothing to her – but to Joe it was everything.

He led Kerry to the middle of the crowded room and held her to him. He snuggled his head into her hair and lost himself in the movement of her body, the fresh smell of her shampoo, the feel of her skin on his. Joe knew then that he had an awful lot to live for.

Not just Kerry. Joe knew it would be wrong to pin all his hopes on her. He had good friends too, people who looked out for him. He had his songwriting and The Loud, he got good grades at college.

He had a bright future. There were to be no more dark days of despair, only hope.

As the song came to an end, they drew apart

and Kerry thanked him, before being tugged away all too quickly by Sonja.

It didn't matter. Joe felt really, truly happy. In fact, he couldn't ever remember feeling this happy before.

Right then he made himself a promise. It might take a week, a month, a year, but one day Kerry would be his.

And when that happened he would never let her go.

Sugar
SECRETS...

...& Lies

SNEAK PREVIEW!

"Anyway, I've got some great gossip for you – this'll take your mind off those stupid things. You know how I went along with Matt to that golf club do last night?"

Kerry nodded. Sonja was meant to have been helping her babysit Lewis but, after a desperate phone call from Matt, had ended up keeping him company instead.

DJing for a bunch of middle-aged golfers in pastel sweaters wasn't exactly Matt Ryan's normal style, but he'd done it as a favour to his father.

Or, to be more exact, his father – who used the club and its members for a little light networking – had threatened to pull Matt's allowance that month if he didn't play ball.

It just cracked Sonja up that Matt had asked her along and not Ollie or Joe – mainly because he didn't want to lose face in front of his mates.

"Well, it turns out Nick's got a new girlfriend!"

"So? Nick's *always* got a new girlfriend," said Kerry, blinking furiously. "Every time we hang out at the café, he's boasting about the latest one."

"Ah, but this time it's different," grinned Sonja knowingly. "He's been going out with this one for three whole weeks and we've heard *nothing* about it! Ollie only found out 'cause he was teasing Nick about how he must have lost his touch.

Anyway, Nick absolutely flipped and said that that was where he was wrong, then just clammed up."

Kerry had to admit that *was* weird. Part of the fun of hanging out at the End-of-the-Line café was hoping that Ollie Stanton's uncle, Nick, would come out from the kitchen and tell them all some long-winded tale or other. These usually revolved around the old rock bands he used to roadie for (everyone featured in the *Guinness Book of Hit Singles*, and more, by the way he spoke), his burgeoning business empire (the café and the second-hand record shop next door), and his success with women.

The fact that he could keep his latest exploit secret was pretty suspicious. And if he wouldn't even tell Ollie what he was up to, well something most definitely was going on.

"And there's more! Apparently, Nick's only gone and joined a gym!"

"What?" gasped Kerry, visualising Nick's belly straining above his tight jeans and thick leather belt with the Rolling Stones logo buckle. A serious diet of egg and chips in the café, and pints of beer in the Railway Tavern with his sidekick Bryan was responsible for that. "Who says?"

"Ollie does," Sonja grinned back, relishing spreading this juicy bit of news. "When he went to open up at the End the other morning, he saw Nick just arriving back from somewhere and go rushing up to his flat with a sports bag. He asked Bryan about it later and he said Nick's been going to that posh gym up at the tennis club every morning lately."

"What do you reckon? Is he trying to lose his love handles for his new girlfriend?" suggested Kerry.

"Nah – I reckon he's met someone there. And I bet it's someone who's not really his type and he's embarrassed being seen with her. You know him – he always likes to have some glamorous young thing on his arm," said Sonja scornfully. "I bet he's seeing some rich, bored housewife or something. Bet this one's some woman in a hideous floral number who thinks Elton John's really rockin'!"

They giggled at the idea of Ollie's uncle trying to hold on to his street cred. Although they all liked him, everyone who hung out at the End thought Nick's taste in music (and fashion) was stuck in a time warp, circa 1975.

Even Matt, who picked Nick's brains on every aspect of the music business, would end up nodding off when Nick went on about ancient bands like Status Quo and Whitesnake, whoever they were.

All the stuff he sold in the second-hand record shop, basically.

"But of course, you realise the saddest thing here," Sonja suddenly sighed. "Whatever's going on with Nick, he's doing a lot better in the romance stakes than any of us."

Kerry nodded. Sonja was right.

"I haven't fancied anyone for so long that I've forgotten what it feels like. And look at Matt! He thinks he's Mr Gorgeous, but he's not exactly fighting them off with a stick. And for all her flirting, Cat's not doing so hot either."

Kerry nodded again as Sonja counted off their crowd on her fingers.

"Maya – well, she's never had a proper boyfriend anyway, and Joe's love-life's a non-starter. Hey!"

Sonja's blue eyes lit up and she turned to her friend with one of those I've-just-had-an-amazing-idea looks that always petrified Kerry. It usually meant trouble.

"Maybe we should get Maya and Joe together! What about it? We could do some matchmaking at the fair this afternoon – bring two beautiful people together..."

"Like *sure*," said Kerry, realising with relief that Sonja was just in wind-up mode. The thought of Maya and Joe together as a couple was about as likely as Posh Spice falling for a Chuckie Rugrat.

A sudden bout of nippy eyes forced Kerry to rummage about in her pocket for another bit of loo roll. She was all out.

Kerry dived into a newsagent's shop.

When she came out, Sonja was leaning against the wall, looking suspiciously thoughtful.

"I was only joking about Maya and Joe," she said, falling into step beside Kerry.

"I know," sniffed Kerry.

"The two people I think should get together are... well, you and Ollie."

Kerry stopped in her tracks and stared at her friend.

"What??!!"

"C'mon – you'd be perfect together," said Sonja, completely ignoring her friend's outrage. "And Ollie's all on his own since Elaine dumped him..."

"Son! What are you on about?"

Kerry was annoyed. Why did Sonja have to say such glib, silly, downright *thoughtless* things sometimes?

She knew full well what had gone on between Elaine and Ollie! They'd parted on good terms a couple of weeks before when Elaine had gone off on a round-the-world trek – and Ollie had decided *not* to go with her.

"I don't know why I didn't think of it sooner!" Sonja continued, ignoring her friend's less-than-ecstatic reaction. "You're both brilliant people – you'd make a really cute couple!"

"Stop it, Sonja! You're just being stupid!" Kerry burst out. "And don't you dare start stirring this afternoon – I know what you're like!"

"But—"

"I mean it!" Kerry warned.

Sonja found herself shutting up for a second time. She hadn't expected Kerry to get so wound up. She'd obviously hit a raw nerve.

Kerry, for the first time that day, forgot about her stinging eyes.

How could Sonja tease her like this? And how could she suggest that she and Ollie could ever be more than just good mates?

She couldn't believe it of Sonja! She was as bad as some of those stupid girls from her sixth-form college who always went on about how boys and girls could never just be friends: that old love thing always got in the way.

Well, they were wrong – all of them. She and Ollie could talk about anything, and she could be her goofy, ordinary self and not feel shy in front of him, as she often did with people. Nope, there was only pure, unadulterated friendship going on between them – no attraction at all.

So yeah, he's cute-looking and everything, but that's never mattered to me, Kerry thought to herself. *I mean, it's not like I could ever imagine myself kissing him, is it?*

DO YOU BELIEVE EVERYTHING YOU HEAR?

● ●

Kerry's so confused right now, she doesn't know what to believe about anything – least of all herself! How good do you think you are at sifting the true from the false?

Look at these scenarios and think about how you'd react if they happened to you...

1. A girl you know is a real show-off. Lately, she's been hinting that the boy you like has a crush on her – but you haven't seen any evidence to back that up. You think...

a) Oh, well, that's my chance blown with him.

b) She's just trying her luck. She thinks if she says it often enough, everyone will believe her – including the boy!

2. Someone tells you that they've heard your boyfriend is still in touch with his ex. You...

(a) Are heartbroken at the very idea. How could he do that to you?

b) Doubt it, and wonder if someone's trying to stir up trouble.

3. You see your boyfriend with his arm round another girl. You immediately think...

(a) It's all over – he's obviously found someone new.

b) It doesn't look good, but there could be a whole load of reasons for what you've seen. You'd give him the chance to do some explaining before you decide whether to dump him.

4. You and your boyfriend are strolling along hand-in-hand, staring into each other's eyes – when your friend comes running along and joins you. You...

(a) Wish she hadn't, but she's your friend, so what can you do about it?

b) Wonder if she's feeling just a teensy bit jealous of the two of you, and deliberately gatecrashed a romantic moment!

5. A girl you know tells you about some trauma going on at home. You've met her family before, and a lot of what she's saying just doesn't add up. You...

a) Feel really sorry for her, and give her lots of attention.

b) Be supportive, but take it with a pinch of salt until you know more.

6. You're meant to meet your boyfriend, but your mate – who's tagging along – turns up so late that you end up missing him. You...

a) Are miserable that it's happened, and want to catch up with your boyfriend as quickly as possible to explain.

b) Wonder if she did it deliberately – because she's jealous about the two of you being together.

7. A friend tells you that she's got a new boyfriend – only you and the rest of your friends have never heard her talk about him before, or ever set eyes on him. You...

a) Think it's a bit weird, but if she's happy, then it's brilliant for her.

b) Have a sneaking feeling that she's making it up.

8. A mate was supposed to pass a message on to your boyfriend for you, but somehow it got all muddled in the telling and came out wrong. You...

a) Don't blame your mate – it's just one of those things. All that's important is sorting things out with your boyfriend.

b) Can't help but think she messed up the story on purpose – either because she's jealous of your relationship, or worse: she's after him herself.

NOW CHECK OUT HOW YOU SCORED...

SCORES

• •

An equal mixture of a and b

You've got an open mind and a trusting nature – but a healthy dose of Sonja Harvey cynicism too! This means that you don't necessarily think the worst all the time: it's just that you don't take people or situations at face value, preferring to think things through before you make up your mind about what's going on, or what a person means.

Mostly a

You might as well have M.U.G. tattooed on your forehead! You're kind-natured but, rather like Kerry, you tend to believe what you see – and that's when the trouble starts. You push doubts to the back of your mind, telling yourself that you're just being silly. But you might find that questioning things a little more might stop you from being used, or getting hurt.

Mostly b

You're not very trusting, are you? In fact, you think everyone's out for themselves – that they're deliberately using half-truths and downright fibs to get what they want. And the reason you think this way is because you're sometimes capable of it yourself – just like Catrina! But using lies to get what you want can be a very big mistake, so think twice before you over-react to a situation in future.

Sugar
SECRETS...
...& Revenge

LOVE!
Cat's in love with the oh-so-gorgeous
Matt and don't her friends know it.

HUMILIATION!
Then he's caught snogging Someone
Else at Ollie's party.

REVENGE!
Watch out Matt – Cat's claws are out...

Meet the whole crowd in the first ever
episode of Sugar Secrets.

*Some secrets are just too good to
keep to yourself!*

Collins
An Imprint of HarperCollinsPublishers
www.fireandwater.com

Sugar
SECRETS...
...& Lies

CONFESSIONS!
Is Ollie in love? Yes? No? Definitely maybe!

THE TRUTH!
Sonja is determined to find out who the lucky girl can be.

LIES!
But someone's not being honest, which might just break Kerry's heart...

Some secrets are just too good to keep to yourself!

Collins
An Imprint of HarperCollinsPublishers
www.fireandwater.com

Sugar
SECRETS…
…& Freedom

FAMILIES!
They can drive you insane, and Maya's
at breaking point with hers.

GUILT!
There's tragedy in store – but is Joe
partly to blame?

FREEDOM!
The price is high, so who's going to
pay…?

*Some secrets are just too good to
keep to yourself!*

Collins
An Imprint of HarperCollinsPublishers
www.fireandwater.com

Sugar
SECRETS...

...& Lust

DATE-DEPRIVATION!
Sonja laments the lack of fanciable
blokes around, then two come along at
once.

MYSTERY STRANGER!
One is seriously cute, but why is he
looking for Anna?

LUST!
Will Sonja choose Kyle or Owen –
or both?!

*Some secrets are just too good to
keep to yourself!*

Collins
An Imprint of HarperCollins*Publishers*
www.fireand**water**.com